# Prisoner

Prisoner Copyright © 2022 by Ellie Kent

All rights reserved.

No part of this book may be reproduced in any form or by any electronic or mechanical means, including information storage and retrieval systems, without written permission from the author, except for the use of brief quotations in a book review.

This novel is entirely a work of fiction, all names, characters, places, and events are the products of the author's imagination, or are used fictitiously. Any resemblance to actual persons, living or dead, events or locations is entirely coincidental.

All rights reserved. Except as permitted under the UK Copyright, Designs and Patents Act 1988.

Ellie Kent asserts the moral rights to be identified as the author of this work.

Ellie Kent has no responsibility for the persistence or accuracy of URLs for external or third party Internet Websites referred to in this publication and does not guarantee that any content on such websites is, or will remain, accurate or appropriate.

Designations used by companies to distinguish their products are often claimed as trademarks. All brand names and product names used in this book and on its cover are trade names, services marks, trademarks and registered trademarks of their respective owners. The publishers and the book are not associated with any product or vendor mentioned in this book. None of the companies referenced within the book have endorsed the book.

First Edition.

ISBN: 987-1739101800

Cover design: © The Pretty Little Design Co

Editor: Lawrence Editing - www.lawrenceediting.com

# Prisoner

KINGS OF THE FIRST DISTRICT *book one*

ELLIE KENT

# *Dedication*

To me, Elsspages, and bookstagram,
this story wouldn't have existed without bookstagram and
the amazing community I've been a part of as Elsspages.
So cheers to that.

# Author's Note

Writing a book was never a dream of mine. On some random day in February 2021, inspiration struck and here we are. The thought of anyone reading this is terrifying, but I know what it's like to be a reader and if my story can make one person react the way I do to my favourite books, then I've already won.

I'm that annoying reader who harasses authors with voice notes, videos, and messages non-stop when I'm reading. Just so you know, I welcome you, and the voice notes, all day, every day. As long as you're happy for me to voice note you back!

I may be the author of this book, but I'm a reader at heart, and I just hope I can give you a form of escapism, or help you find your next book boyfriend...

He's definitely one of mine.

Peace and love.

AUTHOR'S NOTE

TWs:
sexual assault, mentions of rape, parental death, mentions of suicide, murder and dubious consent.
If any of these are triggers for you please proceed with caution.

# Playlist

Centuries - Fall Out Boy
I See Red - Everybody Loves An Outlaw
Watch Me Burn - Michele Morrone
Cravin - Stiletto, Kendyle Paige
Hunger - Ross Copperman
Throne - Bring Me The Horizon
Give Em Hell - Everybody Loves An Outlaw
Hear You Me - Jimmy Eat World
Drink Me - Michele Morrone
Do It For Me - Rosenfeld
Devil Side - Foxes
Blood On A Rose - Everybody Loves An Outlaw
Can You Hold Me - NF, Britt Nicole
Shameless - The Weeknd

# Prologue
## Theo

Through the trees, I can make out his tall frame, his muscles bulging through his shirt and his big head. His stupid, big fucking head that's blown with ego and secrets.

He swaggers towards the cars with what's clearly an exaggerated limp, surrounded by his circle of bodyguards, the outline of his gun on show in the belt holder off his right hip.

The most notorious leader of them all: Carlo Rhivers. He runs the First District, overlooking the Second and Third like a king on his throne. Everyone within the Three Districts fears him.

Except for me.

Not anymore.

Which is why I'm going to kill him. Right here. Right now.

I grip the handle of my pistol until my knuckles go white, my palms slightly clammy, my knees desperate for relief to rise from the crouching position I've been in for roughly half an hour and get the blood flowing. I triple-check that the bullets are in place. I can't fail at this. This is my only chance.

My only chance to murder the man who murdered my mother.

And I'll be damned if he doesn't feel my wrath.

# 1.
# *Theo*

### Two years before

I scream.

The sound pierces the air, travelling over the hills and lakes that surround the Second District. Jumping into the bath, I hold my mother close, trying to will life back into her.

She's submerged under the water, cold and shrivelled, her lips nearly completely blue.

Not the light blue painting the sky, or the blue in the ripples of a waterfall, but the pale blue that hints at a bruise on pale skin.

Who knows how long she's been here.

When I got back to the house after being out all day, it was eerily quiet. All the lights were off. The only light was the flickering of a candle coming from under the bathroom door.

I assumed my mother was just taking a relaxing bath. I called out a hello and left her there, not waiting for a response. She deserves to relax. It's hard enough work being the daughter of a district leader, let alone being married to one.

My father, Kennedy Harlow, a balding man with new wrinkles every day from the stress of his position, became the leader of the Second District when my grandfather passed. I was young at the time, and for as long as I can remember, my dad's been the one in charge.

He's not a bad father, but he's nowhere near a good one either.

He loves two things in this world with his whole heart. His wife and his reputation. There isn't time to care about me. It used to be hard to accept, but now I'm used to it.

It is what it is.

WALKING THROUGH THE OPEN HALLWAY, *on the opposite end of the corridor where I left Mum relaxing in the bath, I push open my large white bedroom door and just like every day upon returning home from training with Emerson, I fall backwards and collapse on my bed.*

*Staring at the ceiling, my legs dangling off the other side of the mattress, I shut off my mind and trace the swirling patterns on the white ceiling.*

*White.*

*Everything is white.*

*The doors, ceilings, walls. The bannister leading up the staircase. The marble flooring in the kitchen and bathrooms. The carpet in all the rooms.*

*Clean and pure. Everything I know my family is not.*

*Sitting up slowly, about to take my boots off, I notice an envelope placed dead centre on my pillow. An envelope with* my name scrawled on it in my mother's neat and cursive handwriting.

Instead of opening it, I make my way to the bathroom door.

"Mum, what's this letter?" I ask, knocking lightly on the door. There is no answer. In fact, there is no noise at all. Only the ticking of a clock coming from down the hallway.

"Mum?"

Still no answer. I gently knock on the door, only for it to open slightly, the door not locked.

Scrunching my brows together, I slowly step inside, the flicker of the candle blowing rapidly with my presence as I brush past it and turn on the light switch. Bright light illuminates the stark white bathroom and that's when I see her.

She looks so peaceful, she could've been sleeping, but I know what she looks like when she's asleep. Her face is always scrunched up and her chest rises and falls quickly, like she's always nervous about being unconscious. Nervous about what could happen to her during that time.

But she isn't asleep now.

No.

She's dead.


I SCREAM.

A scream that pierces the air, travelling over the hills and lakes that surround the Second District.

I stumble, losing my footing on the bath mat, and knock the candle from where it was perched on the edge of the sink. Fire spreads up the drapes, surrounding the window, and panic sets in.

I start pulling at it, trying to rip the curtain down to stamp out the fire. Flames lick my arms, the heat attacking my flesh in my attempt, and more screams surface from deep in my throat.

The drape falls down and I quickly stamp on it—fortunately, I'm still wearing my boots. The fire is out quickly, not having spread further, but my lungs heave in the smoke it caused, burning down my throat, my arms still ignited from the sensation the flames had left.

I turn back to my mother's lifeless body, lying there in the freezing bath water, and scream again. My hands reach into the water and I bite out a groan as the cool water covers my singed arms.

Holding my mother's cold, lifeless body in my arms causes me to shut down. I scream and scream until my throat is raw and there's nothing left in me. No more sound comes.

The tears are uncontrollable as they stream down my face. The sobs, once loud and deafening, are now a whimper.

I don't know how long I stay there. It could be minutes or hours, but I come to my senses when I hear the front door bang open and heavy footsteps racing up the stairs.

"Dad" I scream, begging for his attention, guiding him to the bathroom. "Dad!"

But it isn't my dad who walks through the bathroom door.

No. It's Carlo Rhivers, the leader of the First District, who barrels through the doorway, taking in the sight before him.

"What are you—Where's my dad?" I manage to say in a shaky voice, completely struck by his appearance. *What the fuck is he doing here?*

Carlo Rhivers is *never* in the Second District unless he's on business with my father. So why is he here now?

"Theodora, let's go," he says, gauging what's happened, trying to reach for my arms that are still firmly around my mother's lifeless body. "Theodora, this is a crime scene. You need to let her go!"

But I can't let her go. I can't. And I'll be damned if I let this man tell me what to do.

As I try to cling on to her, strong arms heave me up. I'm hauled away from the bath and away from my mother. I kick and scream, but no matter how much I fight, I cannot shake them.

Once we're away from my mother, I'm put down on the ground and into someone's arms. The scent of my father invades my senses and I continue to break down whilst he holds me, my wet clothes soaking through one of his ridiculously expensive suits that he always wears.

"Where were you?" I scream at him, angry that he let this happen even though I know it's not really his fault. There's no way of knowing if he even knew or not.

But he says nothing. He just looks at me, at my arms, and at the big white bathroom door. Blank eyes. Unseeing.

I collapse on the ground next to him, shielding my arms and crying into the floor, my wet clothes leaving a dark wet patch on the pristine white carpet.

I'M IN THE BATH, the same bath my mother's life ended. Just hours ago, her death was released as *breaking news* in the press.

**'Kennedy Harlow's wife commits suicide'**.

They didn't even write her name. Even in death, she's another possession. It's just another news article on Kennedy Harlow, the precious District Leader.

They say she committed suicide. That being Kennedy Harlow's wife became too much, so she chose the easy way out.

It's bullshit.

My mother was happy and my father loved her very much. He chose her when they were young and even with his lifestyle, she accepted his proposal. They were in love. Real love.

And she had me. She loved me. She'd never leave me.

As cliché as it sounds, my mother was my best friend. My only friend really. And like all best friends, I knew her.

I could tell what she was thinking by her facial expressions, and we could communicate with just one look. We'd never let each other down or stop protecting the other.

And that's why I know there is no way it could have been suicide.

My mind wanders back over the day I found her, trying to make sense of it, when I remember the envelope.

Shit, was it a suicide note after all?

The thought hadn't crossed my mind, and after the police left and everybody left the house, I'd totally forgotten about it.

I jump out of the bath, the water sloshing over the edges as I run from the bathroom across the hall to my room without bothering to grab a towel. I'm the only one home anyway.

The door slams shut behind me when I enter my room, and I run to the far corner to rip off the loose skirting board, little bits of dust dirtying up the white carpet. Reaching in, I pull out the envelope that I stuffed in there quickly before anyone could find it and take it from me. The police weren't taking the last words I'd ever receive from my mother.

A shiver wracks through my naked body and I run to the wardrobe, take out the black silky robe, and shrug my shoulders into it, carefully sliding the fabric across my scarred arms.

Lucky for me, the burns hadn't done too much damage and hadn't affected any of my nerves, just left behind some scarring that the doctor said may even disappear completely after a few years.

I walk over to my dresser, the large vanity built into the wall, next to the open window that overlooks the garden and pool. Some of the staff attend to the greenhouses and plants, sprucing it up for the summer.

Spring is my mother's favourite time of year. The grass grows longer, and flowers bloom. And she always said she loved to wake up with the birds singing. Fitting really that she dies just as spring comes to an end.

I shut my curtains, shrouding myself in darkness, and turn the envelope in my hands.

Carefully tearing the seal, I pull out the small, folded note. In my mother's dainty handwriting, just a few small sentences fill up the blank space.

*My Theo,*
*Promise me one thing. Never eavesdrop on a conversation not meant for you to hear, my darling. There will always be consequences.*
*My beautiful Theodora. I love you.*

*Fuck.*

This isn't a suicide note. It's a warning.

---

A WEEK LATER, my mother's funeral is in full swing.

Carlo Rhivers and the majority of the First District are in attendance, along with some of the members of the Third District. Although I don't know why they're here—we rarely have anything to do with the Third District. But I suppose they have to show unity and respect for the rest of the District members when something major happens. Keeps the peace, I guess.

The Three Districts make up Newlands, to ensure the country runs smoothly and efficiently. Only these Districts are run by very important but very dangerous people.

People like Carlo Rhivers. People like my father.

Not everyone in Newlands is a part of the Three Districts. There are many people outside, living normal lives away from the life of crime and secrecy, but everyone knows about them. Whether you're brought up in the Districts or outside of them, everyone knows that Carlo Rhivers is in charge and no one stands in his way.

The Three Districts aren't run like your average town or city. The mafia deals with everything here.

They pay with secrets, blackmail without mercy, and kill for punishment.

And there's nothing anyone can do about it.

Not me, not my father, and not the rest of Newlands.

Being shunned by the population of those outside of the

Districts, we're basically our own separate country. The same coin, but two different ways of living.

After a long hour of fake sympathy from people I don't know nor care about, the funeral is over and the masses of people scatter as they head to the Harlow mansion for the wake.

I don't want to go.

An army of that many powerful District families all under one roof is not my kind of fun.

I stand alone at my mother's freshly filled grave. My black knee-length dress sways slightly with the wind, the long sleeves covering the healing skin on my arms. I flick back my long hair—as deep and rich as dark chocolate—so it falls down my back, curling at the ends, the baby hairs that fall over my face blowing into my eyes with the breeze. My usual tanned face is pale, the shadow of a ghost replacing my usual stoic expression.

My cheekbones hurt from false smiles at strangers and my eyes burn, the sting a fresh reminder not to let a tear fall in front of these people. I refuse to cry in front of Carlo Rhivers and his cronies again.

Especially with King and Dax Rhivers mere feet away.

King Rhivers, Carlo's only child, and the heir to the First District, stands tall, much taller than Carlo himself. His dark hair, the same shade as mine, is short and ruffled as if he brushes his slender fingers through it often. The black fedora hat he never seems to be without sits casually under his muscled arm. He wears a black three-piece suit, his shirt undone a couple buttons from the top, tattoos peeking out on his chest, his tattooed hands hidden in his pockets.

I pry my gaze away from his body, straight into his dark

green eyes that are staring right at me with such intensity, I feel a flicker of an ember start to ignite a fire inside my chest. My pulse picks up and my heart stutters as I look into his eyes and remember the boy he used to be. My palms go clammy and a thin sheen of sweat beads on my back as he continues to watch me.

His cousin Dax also trains his eyes in my direction when he notices King not paying any attention to what he was saying.

Some would say King and Dax are yin and yang.

King is dark, handsome, and dangerous, whereas Dax is his opposite with light blond hair that's wavy on top, broad like King, but he carries it in a different way. Plus, he smiles more. Well, more than King anyway, but then King doesn't smile at all, not anymore. Although related and always together, you'd never see the resemblance.

They don't deserve an ounce of my time or attention. In all my twenty-three years of life, King Rhivers has only affected a fraction of it. A fraction that felt so right but proved to be so wrong and since then I've had no reason to interfere with either of them.

Not that my father lets me anywhere near the business side of things. Which is inconvenient considering business is all he does.

But while both King and Dax together are intimidating, they don't scare me like they probably should. He lost my fear all those years ago. He lost any ounce of emotion from me.

I turn from them, bored of King's glares, and head towards the house, my heart rate returning to its normal pace.

Taking the longest route back to the mansion, I make my way to the back entrance of the kitchen to avoid the front door and as many people as possible when hushed voices stop me in my tracks. I can't hear what they're saying, but I step tentatively ahead, peering down the alley where the large outdoor bins are.

Sensing my presence, the whispers stop and Carlo Rhivers stares right at me, a malicious smile playing on his lips.

I try to look innocent, that I stumbled upon them by accident, which in fact, I did.

Carlo approaches me, the man he was involved in the whispered conversation with one step behind him.

"Theodora, what are you doing out here?" Carlo asks as if it's absurd to be seen around the grounds of my own house.

I glare at him.

"Just taking a walk. Around my house..." I pause. "What about you? Why are you hiding out here talking and not inside with everyone else?"

I'm not sure where the confidence or stupidity came from, but I spat it out before it was too late to take it back.

Carlo raises an eyebrow, shock washing over his face momentarily before he narrows his dark eyes and leans in, his scent a ghastly rich cologne, his breath stale as he whispers, "Never eavesdrop on a conversation not meant for you to hear, Theodora. There will always be consequences."

I freeze and keep my face stoic, but the impact of his words hit me like a sudden gust of wind, caught up in a tornado.

Pulling back, something shines in his eyes as he brings his hand up to my shoulder. Squeezing just a little too tightly, he says in a normal pitch, "I'm sorry for your loss," then nods at his crony and they leave me standing there in the small alleyway alone.

There's no denying what he was telling me. He didn't know my mother had written those very same words to me on a piece of paper the day she died. Piecing some of the puzzle together, my mother must've overheard something she wasn't supposed to hear and she paid the consequence. And although I didn't hear what Carlo was talking about, I know he'll be watching and maybe eventually come for me.

But he won't know I'm coming for him.

# 2.
# *Theo*

### Present day

My hands shake slightly from the cold. The tips of my numb fingers still hover over the trigger of my .357 magnum revolver. An all-black, small enough pistol that my father gave to me a few years ago as a precautionary measure.

"*Because of my line of work, Theodora, it's important you keep this with you just in case you ever need it,*" he'd said.

What he really means is '*I'm a criminal and run with the mafia, so the likes of you getting attacked are probably quite high.*' But sure, let's call it work.

Not that I have ever needed it until now, but I made sure during my regular training sessions with Emerson that when the time came, I'd know how. It was Emerson who taught me how to fight and shoot properly. Ever since I was sixteen and my father put that pistol in my hand, I've been an exceptional shooter. Emerson could never believe how easy I'd taken to it.

But it's very rare I even get out of the house, especially in the two years since my mother died. I never had much of a social life before. It was always training and then keeping to myself, usually by reading. But as soon as my dad stopped me from doing anything, life got tedious.

Living within the white walls of the Harlow mansion, having the revolver became irrelevant.

The thought used to haunt me, possibly killing, physically murdering someone with it. How could I live with the blood of someone else on my hands? I'd be no better than my father or the likes of Carlo Rhivers.

But since my mother was murdered, I'd never wanted it more.

Now all I see is red.

I want the blood shed on *my* hands this time.

I'm not haunted by the thought of taking a life anymore. I'm haunted by the thought of failing.

My legs feel weak as the blood circulation is cut off from my crouched position, but I daren't move a muscle. One minor movement will alert them I'm here and until my bullet is inside Carlo, being caught is something I cannot afford.

I look down at my watch and realise it's been nearly thirty minutes. My body is starting to feel the cold air and even though it's still pretty warm this time of year, the evenings are much colder than they were at the beginning of summer.

The old, abandoned warehouse is only seventy to eighty yards ahead of me, lit up in an orange glow by a couple of street lamps that barely have any life left in their bulbs.

Over the course of the thirty minutes I've been crouched here, I've clocked a handful of men patrolling the building, all dressed in black with huge, heavy guns, ready to unleash bullets on any trespassers.

Carlo Rhivers is hosting his termly meetings with the other two Districts. Being bored, alone, and curious in the house, I was able to move around invisible when it suited me and I'd eavesdropped many times outside of my father's office despite my mother's warning.

I've picked up some useless information many times, but I've also learned some helpful, interesting, or disturbing information. For example, Carlo holds termly meetings, each time at a new location to maintain anonymity, but local enough for everyone to travel to and always within the Three Districts so no one travels into Newlands.

My father and his men are amongst the group. King and Dax will be there too.

Theodora Harlow, however, is not and will not ever be invited.

Why? Because I don't have a dick.

*"These meetings are no place for a girl, Theodora."* My father's words replay in my head.

Girl my ass. I've probably got bigger balls than him.

Not that he showed me an awful lot of attention previously, but since my mother's passing, Kennedy Harlow has treated me like an inconvenience and an incompetent little girl.

He still believes Mum's death was suicide. Whether he really believes that or is too scared to do anything about my accusation against Carlo, I'll never know.

After my confrontation with Carlo in the shadows at my house, I'd told my dad that Carlo had done it. That *he* murdered my mother. But he didn't listen, not once. He said I was grieving and wanted to blame someone. After months of trying to get through to him, I gave up. I couldn't show him the note my mother left me, so I had no proof to back up my accusation either.

But according to dear old Dad, if she couldn't handle this life, then apparently neither can I, therefore I've been left in the dark for two long years, but what my father doesn't know is that I've been training and plotting for this moment right here.

Emerson, although only a few years older than me, was appointed head of 'Theo security' by my father after my mother passed, but long before that he was my trainer and my friend. He's been teaching me to fight, to respond, how to use a gun since I was in my teens.

Emerson is a beefy guy and happened to be employed by my father's ranks when he turned eighteen. His father used to work for him but when he passed and Emerson was growing up with his auntie, Kennedy Harlow saw an opportunity and took it.

Our relationship doesn't stray from training and the odd conversation anymore. Twenty-year-old Theo had seduced him one night and used him as a get out of jail free card, to take her virginity and 'show her what she was missing'.

It wasn't anything special, but it was in a way, a metaphorical kick in the teeth to the guy who was supposed to take it and a stab in my father's back, who thought his Theo security was a loyal henchman.

But, as I should have anticipated, when it comes to me, my father doesn't even notice anymore.

I'm an incompetent, inconvenient, invisible little girl. We rarely speak unless he's dismissing or insulting me.

But it has worked in my favour. His obliviousness to me is why he has no idea I heard him arrange his car for tonight to attend the District meeting about how the 'confidential business deal' was going and why he has no idea I was on my motorcycle, with the headlight off, speeding down behind him in the distance, following him to his destination.

I wasn't overly fond of my motorcycle. I would've preferred to have driven my little Nissan convertible, but I knew it would be too obvious. Emerson, being my teacher in many things, had taught me how to ride a motorcycle a few years back when I was bored. Once he'd bought a new one, he gave me his old one 'just in case'.

I'd cut off the engine at the end of the road that I knew led to the abandoned warehouse. Leaving it hidden in the bushes, not worried one bit if I never saw it again, I'd crawled most of the way up the dirt path, hidden in the shadows, before taking my place not far from the entrance, but far enough to not be seen.

Now I know I'm not incompetent like my father believes and I know how stupid and practically impossible this is going to be. A young, problematic girl attempting to murder the leader of the First District.

The boss man.

The most protected man in thousands of miles.

The man many capable men have tried to kill and have never succeeded.

But I have no choice but to try. Carlo Rhivers killed my mother. He took any kind of life I had left to live away from me, leaving me without a caring family, scars on my arms, and a hole in my heart.

Carlo Rhivers needs to pay, and I'm willing to pay the price.

After another ten minutes or so, movement piques my interest, and like a deer caught in headlights, my attention is focused sharply at the noise as I hear the wooden door make a deafening creak in the silence.

The men patrolling the area relax slightly and move aside, letting the small crowd of people stumble through. Edison Ramon, the leader of the Third District, appears first with another man behind him, his hood pulled up and head bowed down.

A couple other men I don't recognise leave the building before my father appears with his head of security, Davidson, a breath behind.

Dax Rhivers follows, his eyes scanning the area, sussing out any potential threats. Fortunately, he pays little attention to where I am, his eyes never resting on my hiding spot.

The atmosphere changes as King Rhivers steps out the small wooden door, bending down slightly to fit through the frame. His left hand pulls up his fedora hat, sitting it on his ruffled hair before his hand returns to sit loosely in his pocket, his right hand occupied with his gun.

I hate that I'm momentarily distracted by his loose collar, the top few buttons undone in that way to give you a sneak peek of his tattooed chest.

The butterflies that are already flying around in my stomach intensify at the sight of King. Although grown into the rough, handsome man he is today, I can still recognise the sad smile of a boy I once thought I knew.

Even through my nerves, King stirs something deep within me.

A loud belly laugh interrupts my distraction as Carlo Rhivers walks out the door, slapping a shorter man on the back as he laughs at something that's been said.

The other men have dispersed to their cars, engines already starting to rumble. Dax leans over a black car from the passenger side door, tapping his fingers lightly on the roof as King leans on the driver's side casually, lighting up a cigar.

And there, in front of me, Carlo Rhivers is left wide-open. There's no one protecting him from my line of sight.

It's now or never.

I click the safety off my gun and hold it up slowly, trying not to make any sudden movements to blow my cover now that I've got this close.

I know my aim is immaculate. I've trained too hard for this to miss.

It's now or never.

My tongue sticks out over my bottom lip in concentration. My breathing steadies as I try to fight the nerves creeping up my spine. I close my right eye and look directly down the barrel of the gun.

It's now or never.

I pull the trigger, the loud bang piercing the silent night. A blaring echo interrupts the peaceful breeze in the trees surrounding me.

I recoil the tiniest bit from the shot, my breathing now rapid, my heart racing.

I stare ahead, the dim light illuminating the scene unfolding in front of me.

Men scatter from their cars. The guards haul their weapons up and aim towards the bushes where the shot was fired from. To where I'm now standing.

King and Dax are still leaning casually against the car, King's cigar puffing between his lips as he witnesses the notorious First District leader drop to his knees.

Carlo's eyes glaze over as his body falls, almost in slow motion, to the dirty ground. The blood trickles into his eyes and down his nose, decorating his suit a crimson red from the fresh bullet wound, right in the middle of his forehead. Delivered by a woman with a vendetta.

# 3. King

I heard the gunshot before I acknowledged what was happening. The adrenalin that surged through me at the noise I'm no longer frightened of but rather excited by rings through my ears. A small smile, one no one would have noticed in the chaos, creeps up my face.

I didn't think she'd actually do it.

I see my father hit the ground.

First his knees.

Then his stomach.

And finally his head, with a fresh bullet wound to finish his descent.

When noticing I'm in no hurry to check on Carlo, Dax makes his way over to him, dropping to his knees at his uncle's side, feeling for a pulse. Which is pointless. Why bother when we all saw the bullet go straight through his skull?

My father wasn't a nice man. Everyone knows that. Being the leader of the First District, having the authority and responsibility to overlook the other two Districts, required him not to be.

Not that I'd grant his death upon him now. I had plans

for my father. Plans that required him dying at *my* hand, when *I* was ready, in the most brutal, painstaking way.

I owe death upon my father through revenge and hate, not at the hands of someone else. They don't deserve that victory.

I hear a rustling from my left and finally look up from my father's dead body to see my father's men, who I guess are *my* men now, bringing a resentful Theodora Harlow from the shadows.

The gun she used is held firmly in the hands of one of the guards, whilst another restricted her hands behind her back.

She isn't fighting them off or trying to get away. She knew this would happen and she's welcoming it.

Her face is set like stone and her eyes never waver from mine. Memories flood through me as I stare deeply into her light blue eyes- those light blue eyes that I've not once been able to get out of my head.

Her dark chocolate hair falls untidily down her back and I remember how it looked curled when wet.

She frowns as I look her up and down, my gaze landing on her lips and, for a brief second, I wish I could taste them again.

Not a chance, King.

"Theodora." I acknowledge her, her name sounding sour coming from my lips after so many years. She stands several feet ahead of me and Dax, who's now at my side. I cross my arms over my chest, not backing away from her stare down. It's cute how she thinks she has any semblance of control here.

A low shout interrupts us and Theodora's eyes scan the

smaller crowd that leaves to follow the sudden noise. Her father rushes over to us, his car abandoned up the gravel path, his door still left wide-open.

"Theodora, what have you done?" Kennedy Harlow shakes her shoulders, anger radiating over his whole body. She turns to look at her father, schooling a little emotion to her features.

"Sorry," she whispers, shrugging her shoulders, barely audible but enough for us all to hear. She doesn't sound very sorry at all.

He removes his hands from her shoulders and balls them into fists at his side. The urge to hit her seems apparent in all his features.

"You fool. This is why you couldn't ever be involved with business, Theo. You're reckless. You're done for," he spits.

Kennedy turns to me, pure disgust written all over his face. He looks down at Carlo, then back at me.

"Take her. She's all yours. I'll be in touch." He walks away back to his abandoned car, without an inch of a fight for his daughter, his only child. I planned on taking her with or without her daddy's permission anyway, but do District leaders have absolutely no love or care towards their children?

Theo doesn't react, not even a little bit surprised or upset over her father's dismissal.

I turn to Dax, who is eyeing Theodora up and down, a confused look on his face as he tries to figure her out.

Understandably.

She did just kill his uncle, my father and the leader of the First District, with seemingly no help.

Maybe I've underestimated her.

When I saw her bike pull into the dirt road through the cameras outlining the property and watched her run for cover, stalking in the shadows, I thought she was just here to eavesdrop or get inside.

Not to murder Carlo Rhivers.

If I'd thought that was the reason she was here, would I have stopped her? Probably not. Even if I'd wanted his blood on my hands. But would I have also believed she could've done it? Not at all.

"Get someone to sort him out." I jerk my head at the lifeless body of my father, throwing my burnt out cigar to the ground. Instantly, a few guys get to work, making calls to take my father's body away.

I step closer to Theodora and speak to my men, but never take my eyes off hers. Unease starts to set in at her calmness and the caveman in me wants to rile her up until she reacts.

"Put her in the car. You know where to take her."

The two guys restraining her nod and start to move her before I reach out and put a hand on her shoulder. She glares at me and spits at my feet, and a small smile pulls at my lips, indulging in the satisfaction.

"You want to know what's going on, sweetheart? You're about to find out." I wink and let go. The men walk her to the car, force her into the back seat, and lock the doors.

The Theodora I used to know is not the same Theodora being hauled away now. I know her father shuns her from any District business and she's barely seen outside of her place since her mother's suicide.

She might not have come here to eavesdrop, but I know she's curious either way.

"Are you sure you want to do this, King? She could tell someone," Dax says cautiously.

"She has no one to tell, Dax. She's ours now. She's not going anywhere."

He nods and we both head back to my Cadillac. I slide into the driver's side as Dax takes the passenger seat next to me. Turning on the engine, I follow the car ahead, heading into the depths of the First District.

I think about Theodora sitting in the back seat, a gun probably trained on her in case she attempts to pull any shit.

But she won't. She knew what would happen when she got caught.

Memories buried deep flood to the forefront of my mind and I think about the first time I saw those blue eyes. But then they remind me how the once shallow pools of her light blue eyes had quickly turned into a deep, dark abyss and my hatred comes back tenfold.

But why was she here now? What was her motive? Carlo Rhivers had many enemies, but how did he make one of Kennedy Harlow's daughter?

The only logical explanation is she did it for her father, but he seemed to have no idea she was here. The way he spoke to her, unless he was all of a sudden an exceptional actor, he definitely wasn't using her as a hitman.

So why?

"You okay, cuz?" Dax speaks up after a few minutes of silence. He must be thinking about Carlo and the situation we've now found ourselves in.

I feel guilty, only for a split second, that I'm wasting my time thinking about the girl in the car in front and not on my father's dead body that's not even cold yet.

"Yeah, man," I respond. "You?"

"Yeah," he replies.

And I know he is.

The District's ours now. The mansion, Districts Two and Three, and even Newlands and all the people in it will know that it all now belongs to *me*.

All of it.

Including *her*.

---

ALMOST AN HOUR LATER, we're driving down the dark country lane. The only light the moon had offered us vanished through the thick trees that create an archway over the road.

Approaching the large, three-storey building, our headlights light up the District jail, secluded and abandoned from life apart from those who know it's there. Or in other words, the three District leaders and their men.

This isn't your average prison, though. The District jail is for those who cause havoc for any of the District members. Liars, cheaters, thieves, thugs, rapists, murderers. Hell, all you have to do is look at a District member wrong and you could end up here for life.

We don't kill these criminals out in the real world. That's too easy of a way out. Instead, they're sent here for punishment. To learn from their mistakes. Not that they can learn and move on.

No one leaves once they're in.

When you enter the cells, you die in the cells whether

it's an accident or on purpose or a natural death from illness or old age.

Many prisoners have killed themselves. Many of them have killed others. It's every man for themselves once you're in.

There hasn't been a new prisoner here for almost a year. It's been quiet in business.

And we've never had a female prisoner before.

Until tonight.

They're in for a right treat.

The car ahead of me stops and I pull up next to them.

"You ready for this?" Dax looks at me and a small grin pulls at my lips.

"Hell yeah!"

# 4.
# Theo

After almost an hour of driving, the car stops. I clock the time on the dashboard before the engine is cut off, noting that it's almost one in the morning.

The two men exit the car, slamming and locking the doors behind them. I undo my seat belt and lean forward slightly between the two front seats to get a better look at the building in front of me.

Lit up only by both cars' headlights, I can see a huge building, with fading paint on the bricks outside. There are no windows or lights coming from inside, and I can't see how far back it goes as tall, thick trees surround it.

Anxiety worms its way into my mind as I discover I'm in very unfamiliar territory.

King and Dax join the two men who were driving me as they stand in the glow of the headlights. They discuss something briefly before Dax makes his way over to my side of the car and I scoot back quickly into my seat, not wanting him to catch me snooping.

The locks click, signalling the cars being unlocked, and my door opens. Dax Rhivers looks down at me as his palm reaches out in front. A soft expression is planted on his face.

His calming nature soothes my anxiety and I'm grateful for it.

I place my hand in his and he helps me out of the car.

As I right myself and stretch out my legs, my arms are yanked back, forcing me against Dax's chest as he handcuffs my wrists together, the calm and gentle nature from before merely a disguise, a sweet trick into easy submission.

Anger creeps its way up to the surface as he manhandles me. He walks me forwards and King replaces Dax's position behind my back, holding my wrists.

The faint aftermath of smoke surrounds him, mixed with a heavenly, masculine cologne of a woodsy aroma and notes of vanilla.

"You ready, sweetheart?" King whispers in my ear.

I cringe away, the slight flutter in my stomach and tingle between my thighs at his whisper an immediate betrayal of my feelings.

"Do your worst." I turn my head and whisper back to him, my lips brushing against the stubble on his jaw. I recoil back at the contact, his scent still overtaking my senses, making me dizzy.

Tightening his hold on my wrists, he yanks me back, pulling me right against his solid chest as his other hand reaches around and holds me by the neck, forcing my head up to meet his gaze.

My heartbeat suddenly picks up, and I pray to God he doesn't feel the speed of my pulse quickening beneath his hand.

"So she speaks," he mumbles, his eyes flickering between mine, his jaw ticking in frustration. Then he drops his forehead to mine. Our eyes lock and he whispers, low, for only me to hear, "You're going to regret that, sweetheart."

He pulls back and pushes me forward so I'm forced to follow Dax, King still right behind me. My back is glued to his chest whilst he guides me by my wrists. At this point, I'm unsure if the other two men are still following.

I watch Dax in front of me, admiring his build. He's tall and muscular, his back rock-solid before meeting a perfect ass, shown off nicely in his suit trousers. I think of King, who to my annoyance is everything Dax is, times ten. His firm hand gripping just a little too tightly on my handcuffed wrists, his other on the small of my back, guiding me. I can feel his warm breath blow against the top of my head. Every now and then, he lets out a low grumble as he clears his throat, and each time my knees weaken a little more. His strong, hard chest, which I know is covered in tattoos, is still unnecessarily pushed against my back as we walk.

After what feels like ten minutes of walking, we approach the dark building I studied from the car. There's still no light coming from inside and no sign of life. The only difference is I underestimated how big it is. It stands tall above me, maybe six or seven storeys high.

We round the corner and approach a single doorway. I'm surprised that nobody is guarding it, seeing as none of the District leaders go anywhere without protection. Dax fishes in his pockets and pulls out a single set of keys, all oddly shaped. I try to catch a glimpse of which key he uses, but it's too dark. The door opens and a burst of light floods the ground and Dax in front. He walks through without glancing back at any of us.

And we follow.

We walk through a brightly lit corridor before stopping at another closed door at the end. My hands are released and King unchains the handcuffs that are starting to dig into my skin. I instantly grab my wrists and rub at them to ease the slight numbness.

The door opens into a large empty room with white walls—nowhere near as clean as the walls back home—and wood tiled floor. King leads me inside as Dax and the other two men follow. *So they're still here.*

Aside from a lone shower head hanging off the wall in the corner, it's completely empty of furniture. I slowly take in the surroundings and try to find a possible way out of this, turning back to the door we came through, but it's sealed shut.

I turn my head back to the four men who are keeping me company in the room and study them as they all stand in a line before me. I feel intimidated and small but refuse to cower. After a painful silence, King crosses his arms across his chest, clearing his throat.

"Strip."

My stomach flips at his voice and I stare at him, trying not to show the surprise and panic I feel from his demand. When I make no movements, he repeats himself.

"Strip."

I shake my head slowly and the corner of King's mouth tips up.

"Sweetheart, if you don't, I will do it for you."

I know he's not bluffing, but I still refuse to move.

So they've brought me here to get me naked and have their way with me. Is that it? King takes a few steps towards me, meeting me in three strides.

"Strip," he commands again, anger clear in his dark green eyes.

But against my better judgement and the angel on my right shoulder, I continue to stand still.

Dax shuffles on his feet whilst the other two men watch eagerly on. After a few moments, King fists my sweatshirt in his hands and rips it to shreds, throwing what remains of it onto the floor at my feet. My skin feels the chill of the room, goosebumps coating my arms at the cold air, my nipples perking up at the change in temperature.

"Are you going to do the rest or shall I carry on?" he asks, cocking a brow.

But again, my stubborn ass doesn't move. Nothing King does will ever frighten me. I won't let him have that power.

His mouth tips up in the corners once again and he turns and walks back to Dax. He pulls Dax's knife out of his holder and returns to his stance in front of me.

King bends on one knee and puts a hand around my calf and lifts it slightly, pulling off my trainer and sock before bringing the knife to my ankle.

I look down at the knife resting on my bare skin under my leggings and then back at King, watching his eyes roam over my body.

My choice of clothing tonight being my baggy sweatshirt and workout leggings had allowed me plenty of room to move about freely whilst I crawled through the bushes only hours ago. Now they feel thin and flimsy under his gaze.

King returns to the task at hand and the blade disappears under the material. The sharp edge of the knife turns outwards, cutting the clothing easily as he slides it up my leg.

The leggings split open as he works the knife all the way up, cutting through the waistband, his eyes never leaving mine as he does. Stopping just inches away from my pussy, my breath hitches before King returns the knife to my other leg and repeats the same process, pausing for just a moment to smile up at me before slicing through the waistband, and what remains of my leggings falls to the floor, leaving me bare in just my bra and knickers.

I daren't remove my stare from his. *This will not affect me.*

Standing up slowly, his breath tickling every inch of my skin, King wraps his arms around me, the knife firmly in his hand at my back, but I still stand frozen.

I hear the rip of material and a slight cold sensation as the knife slices through my bra, the blade placed flat against my shoulder blades for a mere moment. My bra stays in place whilst King stands in front of me. He looks down at the material that's barely covering my breasts before looking back up at me, a salacious grin covering his face.

I see the glint in his eye before King steps back, my bra falling with him as I'm bared for everyone to see, my nipples hardening further as the cold air hits them. I don't take my eyes away from King, but in my peripheral vision, I can see Dax's head bent to the ground, but the other two men are still staring, way too eager.

King goes to move the knife under my panties, but I grab the flat edge of the blade before he gets there.

"I'll do it," I say, jutting out my chin. *I'll keep what little dignity I have left, thank you.* I hook my fingers under my knickers and pull them slowly down my legs, bending with them before stepping out and standing fully naked for the men to feast their eyes on, apart from Dax who is still more interested in his shoes.

King looks me up and down slowly, a look of adoration mixed with hunger, and the heat between my legs pools again. I curse myself for letting his gaze affect me after what he's just done to me.

King jerks his chin in the direction of the shower and I look at it over my shoulder before looking back at King. Rolling my eyes, I walk over to it and a shrill scream escapes my lips as the spray hits me automatically once I position myself underneath the head. I stand under the icy water, shivers wracking my body instantly, and I take short gasps of breath as my body tries to get accustomed to the cold.

My skin turns a pale white, the goosebumps now erratic and all over my body. My nipples are steel points that are painful under the jets. I tilt my head down, tucking my chin into my chest as my hair falls over my face, curling under the spray of the water.

Once he's satisfied, King's voice fills the silence.

"Come."

I lift my head and turn to see Dax has opened another door on the opposite side of the room and I walk through, dripping wet, following him. King at my back once again.

Suddenly, I'm self-conscious about my nakedness around two of the most eligible bachelors of the Three Districts and I hug my arms over my breasts to keep some decency.

After being ushered down another long corridor, wet footprints in my wake, we walk out into a huge open space.

There are cells on both sides of the room that go up another few storeys. It's some proper *Shawshank* shit.

I continue to follow Dax, but our presence has obviously disturbed the occupants of these cells, which are most definitely *not* empty, and suddenly there are yells, whistles, and catcalls coming at me from every direction.

I scan my eyes all around, seeing man after man occupying hundreds of cells, running their eyes all over my naked body. I try to hug my arms tighter around myself to cover my body, but King grabs an arm, pulls it away, and gives me a warning look.

Fear takes over as I try to make sense of everything.

We go up one flight of cold metal stairs and then I'm pushed into a stone grey cell accommodated with one towel, a dirty charcoal jumpsuit resting on a mattress, and a pair of threadbare socks with black pumps to complete the outfit. Glancing to my right, I see a small metal toilet bowl and sink, both in view of any peeping toms.

I grab the towel quickly and cover myself before turning to King as the cell door slams closed, the keys clanging together as Dax locks me in, a short apologetic look in his eyes that had I blinked, I would've missed.

"Sleep well, sweetheart." King winks before all four men who brought me here disappear.

So they run a prison. *This* is the big District secret my father kept hidden from me. A voice shouts out to shut up the other prisoners from their yells and catcalls, and I'm left alone in my new cell, ready to be their newest prisoner.

# 5. King

"Are you sure you want her in here?" Dax asks, nursing his glass, swirling the ice around the brown liquid.

"Why wouldn't I?" I respond blandly.

Dax scoffs. "You're kidding, right? You know those cell doors open in the morning. She'll be vulnerable to every sick fuck in there," he spits, using his arm to point dramatically back out to the door from which we just came.

Dax is rarely angry. He seems to be at peace with where he is in life. He's found his girl, went through hell to get her, but he got her nonetheless. He's happy being my accomplice, my right-hand man. He doesn't want the leadership, the responsibility. He never did. He's content and surviving.

So when he's angry, you know he's about to lose his shit.

"You can't treat women like this, King. They don't deserve it."

"Don't deserve it?" I spit back, turning from the large-scale window I was staring aimlessly through. It's the only window in the building, and it isn't visible from the front.

"The bitch shot my father. Your uncle!" I point at him.

Dax stands up from his seating position and strides over to me. "I know, King, but there are other ways we can punish her instead of leaving her unprotected in that shit hole. And don't act like she didn't do you a favour either. We all wanted Carlo dead, so stop acting like it's a big deal just because she got there first. And don't give me that *he's my father* bullshit. Blood means shit and you know that."

"Blood means shit, does it? So what does that mean for us then, *cousin,* hmm?"

Dax pauses, realising what he's said without intending to.

He lets out a low, exasperated sigh and puts his drink down on the glass table. He approaches me, placing both hands on my shoulders.

"You know I didn't mean it like that, King. Look, I've got your back. Ride or die, innocent or guilty. Blood related or not, that wouldn't change. Do what you have to do, just for the love of God, think about your choices carefully."

I nod. I know what he says is true—to an extent.

Dax leaves, turning back to nod once more. I face the window of the study, looking out into literally nothing. The dark, thick trees block any kind of view, and the only thing visible is the slight moonlight spying through the branches.

I place my hat back on my head and pocket the cigar I never ended up lighting. Dax has fucked up my thought process. I never thought about her safety. It didn't even cross my mind. Why would it?

But when those cells unlock in the morning, every prisoner in there knows where she is. It's no secret that we had brought our new shiny female prisoner in hours ago. And these are prisoners who haven't set eyes on a female in *years.* Hell, some of them in *decades.*

Without a second thought, I drain the rest of my glass and leave the small study with one location in mind.

I'll check on her. That's it.

Making my way through the large steel door, I unlock it and click it back into place as quietly as I can. It was hours ago we came in. Now it's nearing close to five in the morning, and everyone seems to be back asleep after the drama.

Good. I don't need any attention on me.

I creep up the stairs and round the railing to her cell. My eyes have adjusted to the dark and I see her small form curled up on top of the mattress.

She's wearing the dirty, shitty, rumpled jumpsuit that hangs loosely on her small frame. Her hands are fisted in front of her face and her eyelids flutter lightly. Whether she's only half asleep, dreaming, or afraid, I can't tell. She looks so innocent. Her tanned skin and plump pink lips, lips that I barely remember the feel of, are the only colour in the whole cell, instantly brightening up the lifeless space.

Looking down at her, I think about the whole evening, thoughts of her naked body at the forefront of my mind. The goosebumps shadowing over her were like a second skin, her chest rising rapidly at the embarrassment, the water cascading down her breasts and stomach, droplets racing each other as they dropped lower. How can I let any of these criminals look at her the same way? Touch her before me?

My spine shivers, the skin on the back of my neck prickles, and I feel eyes on me. I look to the left and see the big, muscular guy in the cell next to hers leaning against the railings, his forearms resting against the rails as his hands hang loosely over the other edge. He cocks an eyebrow at me and a smile plays at my lips.

He nods in the direction of Theodora, never breaking my eye contact. I look back at her sleeping form, then back at her neighbour. I nod back, placing my hand in his and giving him a small handshake.

Then taking one last look at Theodora, I walk away, leaving her in this hell hole.

## 6.
## Theo

I jolt awake, the horrid dim lighting giving nothing away as to what time it is. It feels like three in the morning, but I know that isn't the case. The time on the dashboard of the car read around 1:00 when I was brought in here.

I sit up, my head throbbing slightly at my disorientation. Scanning the small space, my eyes stop on a man sitting on a stool by the doorway to the cell. On the inside of the *locked* cell, might I add.

He's big and muscular, barely fitting into his dull jumpsuit, which makes me wonder if they're one size fits all. No one would challenge him, though. From what I can see, his skin is covered in ink and his hair is cropped short. He looks around twenty-eight, just a few years older than me.

The intruder leans forward, his elbows resting on his knees as he stares at me. I immediately want to panic but then consider the point of that. What would I do anyway? Scream? There's no one coming to my rescue here.

I shuffle my position to mimic his, tucking my legs under myself, my elbows resting on my knees, although I'm a lot less intimidating than his bulky frame. The corner of his mouth tugs up and his whole facial expression turns to one of warmth.

"I like you already," he says in a husky voice, piercing the silence.

Now that I've heard his voice, I'm very aware of all the sounds surrounding me. Metal clanks, voices, deep shouts, and laughter all echo through the walls. I try to look through the bars around the man sitting in my cell.

"The doors open at sunrise. At least we assume it's sunrise," he says again. My eyes find his and they flicker with slight anxiety.

*The doors open?*

"That's how you're in here," I state the obvious.

He nods.

"Either me or all of them," he says, pointing over his shoulder.

The fear eats away at me. My cell is open for anyone to come through? He stares intently at me as I fidget, getting to my feet and pacing slightly around the small space.

"And who's to say you're any better?" I rush out in my panic.

"I'm not going to hurt you."

I stop and look over at him. He's now on his feet and has taken a small step towards me. He reaches a hand out in front of him, between us.

"I'm Puck."

I hesitate. How do I know he won't hurt me? I'm trapped in an unlocked prison cell, with nothing to protect myself, surrounded by criminals who have been locked up for who knows how many years. And for who knows what reasons.

A shorter man in the same matching jumpsuit walks past

and halts when he locks eyes with me. He has greasy, long hair and a few missing teeth. He backs up and reaches out to open the large metal door, and my heart rate picks up once again.

Puck turns to see him and tenses, making his way to the bars that are separating us from him. The smaller guy freezes and backs up into the railing behind him, lifting his hands in surrender before stumbling away.

Puck turns back around and places his hand out in front of him again like nothing has happened. Assessing the situation, an ally would be ideal, especially one the size of Puck. The way he just scared that guy away is proof enough for now that he won't hurt me—yet.

I take his hand in mine.

"Theo," I reply quietly.

He smiles at me, a genuine smile that I thought a place like this would rid you of. "Nice to meet you, Theo."

I return his smile. "Is it?" I ask, dropping my hand and cocking an eyebrow.

"Well, I suppose not under these circumstances, but I'll take the chance to talk to a pretty girl over these assholes any day," he replies, pointing a thumb at those who live behind the bars. I sit back down on my mattress as he takes a seat on the stool.

"That wasn't in my cell," I state, gesturing to the stool he's perched on.

"It's from mine," he replies, nodding to the left. "I'm next door."

"I came in as soon as the bars unlocked," he admits.

I ponder what he's said for a moment. "Why?" I question.

"Because I knew it would be a matter of minutes before one of these fuckers would come in and rape you."

I wince slightly at his brutal honesty.

"I've been in here for nearly an hour or so. You didn't stir once. It would have been too late for you to protect yourself, if you could, by the time one of them came for you and then way too late when their buddies joined in. I'm not a monster. I may be in here, but I respect women and I wouldn't let the awful things they'd want to do to you happen," he states matter-of-factly.

I'm stunned. I go over his words in my head for a few minutes. Thinking of the awful things that could have happened, I get angry with myself for not waking up to the noise or for not noticing there was someone in the cell with me. I focus on one part of his statement more than the others.

"If you're not a monster, then why are you in here?" I ask curiously.

"Why are you?" he challenges.

I smile at his comeback. "I shot Carlo Rhivers in the head," I say sweetly.

He narrows his eyes at me, trying to figure me out. I can tell he doesn't know whether to believe me.

"Pinky swear," I add with a smile, extending my arm and putting my pinky finger out for him to take like a child. Humouring me, he hooks his baby finger, which is the size of my index finger, with mine and laughs.

"Damn, maybe you can handle yourself!"

I laugh back. This situation is fucked up, but at least for now I feel safe with Puck.

"So, big man, why is everyone afraid of you in here?" I saw how the other cellmate responded to him instantly and he wouldn't have put himself in my cell if he couldn't protect me.

"Been here a long time. I earned the respect I got, protected myself and anyone who protected me back."

"How long have you been in here?"

"I lost count after a few years. There's no sense of time in this place. It just is what it is," he said with a shrug.

My heart hurts a little for him. He seems too good a person to be in here, but then again so am I, right? A sharp whistle pierces the area, followed by a loud male voice.

"Shower time!"

My eyes widen as I panic again. The humiliation of walking to my cell naked in the early hours of this morning clouds my thoughts.

Puck stands up and holds his hand out to me.

"I got you. Pinky swear." He smiles.

Well, if I have to trust anyone right now, I may as well trust Puck. He's the best hope I have.

I place my hand in his, grab the towel from the dirty floor, and let him lead me out of the protection of the cell bars that are caging me in. He walks into his cell and grabs his towel off his mattress, never once letting go of my hand. His cell looks identical to mine, apart from marks and words scraped into the walls and the stool that he's placed back in the corner.

He turns us back around and walks us towards the stairs. Men of all shapes and sizes in a sea of grey jumpsuits walk in all directions. Some behind, following us, and some leading.

I scan my surroundings, looking for an exit, but only see cell after cell and man after man. Hungry eyes roam over my body, taking me in, drinking me in with their gazes. I feel dirty under their looks and I inch closer to Puck.

We walk through a doorway that leads to a huge open shower room. Men are undressing out of their jumpsuits and washing themselves in the open showers.

I've seen a man naked before. But to see this many naked men all in one space makes me uncomfortable.

Most of them have turned and found themselves amongst the presence of a female and their gazes fall down my body as they shower, their hands stroking themselves at the thought of my being here. Bile rises up my throat. *I can't do this.* Did they really expect me to shower in front of these men?

But before I even finish asking myself that question, I already know the answer.

Of course they do. They have no respect—they proved that after stripping me off and making me walk naked through the cells.

"I got you," Puck whispers again, sensing my uneasiness. He leads us to the corner of the room and nods at the guy occupying the shower to move. He scurries off and Puck drops my hand, taking my towel out of my grasp. He opens the towel and stretches it out between his arms behind his back, which is facing the corner.

Realising what he's doing, I step behind the towel, looking around from all perspectives.

"Step back," I whisper and Puck takes a step back.

I'm caged in. It's a small space to shower in, but it's as private as I'll get. Double-checking that there are no gaps, I unzip my jumpsuit, step out of it slowly, and hang it up on the hook just on the other side of Puck's outstretched arm.

Puck could easily drop the towel and expose me, but I trust him. Besides, what choice do I really have?

I hit the button on the wall and cold water streams directly on top of me. I hold back a gasp and try to get used to the freezing spray. Once accustomed to the temperature of the water, I grab the small bar of soap, trying not to cringe at all the hands that must've touched it before me, and lather it up in my palms. I run my hands all over my body and through my hair over and over again.

Ridding myself of the dirt and smell.

Ridding myself of the looks these prisoners give me.

Ridding myself of the look King gave me the night before.

Once satisfied, I turn off the water, and Puck passes me his towel, considering mine is still protecting me from prying eyes. I quickly dry and step back into my jumpsuit.

"Thank you," I say, feeling grateful for his kindness and a little guilty at the trouble he's having to go through for a stranger. He turns and holds my chin.

"You're welcome, T."

"T?" I question the new nickname.

"More badass." He shrugs. I laugh at him as he gives me a cheeky smile back. Puck hands me the towel and then unzips his jumpsuit. I sneak a peek at his torso. Rock-solid abs intimidate me as I stare. Before realising it, he's stepped out of his jumpsuit, hung it up, and is standing stark naked in front of me, hiding himself in his hands.

"Keep your eyes off the goods, T." He winks and steps under the shower. "And don't go anywhere," he says from under the spray of the water.

I smile despite the awkward situation I'm in. I face the

wall, staring at the brick so I don't have to see anything unpleasant. Puck laughs as he showers.

"Oh, T, what are we gonna do with you?"

I just continue to smile at the wall.

After Puck showers, we walk back to our cells, him holding tightly onto my hand. We both step into my cell and drop down on my mattress.

"I'm starving," I hum and my stomach starts to rumble.

"Well, you'll be starving for a little while longer. We don't get served food until a little later on. And it tastes like shit, so don't get too excited."

I groan at the hunger, the situation, and the fact I'll never get to eat a decent meal ever again.

"If you had to eat one meal for the rest of your life, better than whatever crap they serve here, what would you pick?"

"Steak. No doubt about it."

"God, you're such a man." I laugh and Puck holds his chest like he's offended.

"Oh yeah, so what about you then?"

"Mac and cheese," I say confidently, ready to defend myself.

"What are you, a twelve-year-old girl?" He laughs, and I slap his arm, knowing his comment was already coming.

"I'll have you know mac and cheese is the gods of all pasta dishes. It's pasta and cheese. Come on!" I defend, not ashamed of my food choices. We sit and laugh over the silliness of the conversation, and I look around the cell and sigh.

"God, this place is such a shithole. Please tell me it gets better than this."

Puck laughs and shakes his head.

"Unfortunately not."

"How do you not get super bored? What do you do for entertainment?"

Puck scoffs. "Entertainment? Theo, look around, there's nothing to do. Unless you want to train with me every day and get some push-ups in?" he waggled his eyebrows. I pull a face and shake my head at the thought of doing push-ups.

"Well, what about all the marks on your wall? What are they?" I ask curiously.

"Just years and years' worth of shit that pops into my head. Names of people I love, words I'm feeling at the time, sentences I remember from random conversations, advice I can remember being given back when I was a lad."

"Advice like what?"

"Silence is full of answers."

I sit and ponder over the meaning, when he chuckles and nudges my arm.

"See, you don't reply and I know what's going through your mind. My father used to say it to me. If I'd done something wrong, broken something and lied about it. I'd never confess and he'd always tell me my silence was full of answers. He was always right too.

"Then he died when I was a teen and my mother could never seem to find the words to tell me and that's when I knew he'd never been more right. Even from your silence now, Theo, I know what you're not saying."

I look up at him and try to find the right words to say, but like he said, sometimes there are no words and silence *is* the loudest answer.

"I'm sorry, I—"

"Forget about it. Now, let's christen this cell of yours, T." He waggles his brows at me.

"What?" I flash my eyes over his face, the sudden change in conversation startling me. I hope he's joking. He chuckles at my reaction.

"Ease up. I meant the walls," he says and flicks a pen knife open that was stashed inside of his jumpsuit.

"Where did you get that?" I ask, sitting up onto my knees, excited at the prospect of having a weapon.

"I run this place, didn't you know?" he retorts sarcastically, although I don't think there was anything sarcastic about it.

He turns around and starts scratching into the brick wall. I watch the muscles in his arm contract with his hard work.

"I don't doubt it after the way everyone's been running away from you. What do you do, kill anyone who looks at you?" I smile as he side-eyes me from where he's carving into the wall.

"Do I look like a serial killer to you?"

I lean back and take in his huge frame and bulking muscles and tilt my head.

"Yes."

Puck stops what he's doing to glare at me and I burst into a fit of giggles.

"Look, T, if you don't want my protection, I can go away, yanno," he says, turning back to his work.

"All right, big man, sorry." I smile. He shakes his head and I leave him to do his thing in peace.

"There," he says after a while, blowing the dust off. He's carved P+T inside a love heart. I guffaw, hitting him on the arm as he pulls me into a headlock.

A strange feeling surges through my whole body. I haven't felt like this since my mother, since *him*. Being happy isn't a feeling I'm used to and finding that here of all places doesn't make any sense. But with Puck, I feel like I have a friend, and that's reason enough for me to smile.

My laugh continues to ripple through my chest as I attack Puck's arm with my hands to escape when a throat clearing startles us and Puck lets me go. We both turn to the cell gate. King and Dax Rhivers stand behind the bars in their pristine suits. King's hat is placed perfectly on top of his head like always. *He looks fucking sinful.*

My smile disappears immediately as I remember where I am. King looks at Puck, his face unreadable, and jerks his head in the direction of his cell. Puck stands up to leave but hesitates slightly when I hold on a little tighter to his arm. Leaning down, he places his hand in front of my face, lifting his pinkie finger up. I hook mine with his, knowing what he's promising.

I'm safe. He's got me. Just like he has all day.

He stands up fully and brushes past King and Dax, nodding at them both as he goes. Dax claps him on the back as he passes and I furrow my eyebrows at the friendly gesture. Once Puck is out of sight, King and Dax step into my cell, closing the bars behind them.

"Theodora." King smiles

# 7. King

I approach Theo's cell, not sure what to expect, but Theo laughing and carefree in Puck's arms isn't it. I lean against the wall in front of the bars, caging her in. Crossing my arms over my chest, I watch her for a few seconds. My eyes narrow at the scene unfolding in front of me.

I thought my intentions were clear last night when I made sure Puck was there to look out for her. And that was all I meant. Look out for her. Not have her in a headlock on her bed, making her smile like that. There's light in her eyes and all her teeth are on show as she laughs with him. An uneasy feeling settles in my stomach.

I've only seen that smile less than a handful of times. Could *I* ever make her smile like that again?

Dax is at my side, but he's not watching them, he's watching me, a glint of something sparkling in his eyes. I shake my head slightly at him, asking him what he wants.

"Jealous, cuz?" he whispers with a smirk. I throw daggers at him with my eyes before turning back to them. But the show in front of me is making me sick to my stomach.

I clear my throat and both of them stop messing around to lock eyes with me. But I just stare deeply into hers. She's uncomfortable. Her eyes falter and I can practically see the cogs turning in her brain, remembering where she is and who put her here.

I break my gaze and look at Puck, jerking my head back in the direction of his cell, hoping he can sense my irritation. Puck doesn't hesitate. He isn't going to disobey me. He never has. Not then and not now. That's why I respect him and trust him with this girl. But maybe I misjudged him. After all, it has been years.

Dax opens the gate, ready for Puck to exit through, when he's brought back down to Theo's level. Her eyes look slightly panicked and the grip she has on his arm is tighter than before. My anger simmers even higher as she seeks out comfort and protection in Puck, this stranger she's known for less than twenty-four hours.

Puck hesitates before lifting his hand in front of them and Theo locks her little finger with his. My brows crease at the personal moment between them. She's only been in here a day. How do they have *a thing* already?

She smiles the smallest bit before Puck turns to leave. He nods at us both, then returns to his cell.

"Theodora." I smile, making my way into her cell. Dax closes the metal bars behind us and the panic in Theo's eyes from when we first arrived is gone. She's back to being a stone-cold bitch. Leaning back against the wall, she glares at me, folding her legs up underneath her.

"How was your first night, sweetheart? I see you've made a friend already." I nod at the wall she's leaning against, indicating Puck. She says nothing. Funny really that she decides to ignore me when I know she has a sharp tongue on her.

"The silent treatment again, is it?" I cock an eyebrow at

her. She rolls her eyes before opening that pretty mouth of hers.

"Don't I get a lawyer or something?" she replies, exasperated. I smile a genuine smile. Even Dax snickers a little.

"Oh, Theodora, that's cute."

"It's Theo," she snaps.

I've been waiting for that reaction. She's rarely called Theodora. Only her father uses her full name. Otherwise, she's known as Theo. But I enjoy pissing her off.

I step towards her, bending down and brushing my hand down her cheek before taking hold of her chin and jerking her head up, forcing her eyes to meet mine.

"I'll call you whatever I want to call you, sweetheart," I whisper.

Her breath catches, her eyes betraying her, showing me a flicker of heat. After a few seconds, she jerks her head back, pulling herself away from my grasp. I stand back and look her up and down.

The oversized jumpsuit drowns her, her figure completely hidden underneath, giving nothing away. Not the size of her boobs, nor her flat stomach or curvy hips.

But I know what she's hiding underneath. My dick swells at the thought of her naked body last night and as if she knows what's going through my mind, her eyes lower to the bulge forming in my trousers. She peeks back up at me from under her lashes, the same heat in her eyes from before returning to them.

I open my mouth to say something, anything, but Dax beats me to it. I forgot he was in the room with us.

"Why did you murder Carlo, Theo?"

She glances over at Dax and I blink away the thoughts

that were running through my mind. This isn't the time or place.

This girl killed my father and she's sitting in a jail cell because of it.

Because I put her here. *Get it together, King.*

Dax's tone is calm and collected, almost friendly, as he questions her.

She clears her throat before simply saying, "Because he's a dick."

Dax chuckles, literally chuckles, at her. I can't take my eyes off her. Does she have a death wish? The audacity of her attitude strikes me.

"Watch your mouth, Theodora," I spit. The use of her full name after requesting I call her Theo doesn't go unnoticed. She stands up and tries to level with me, which is impossible as I have a good few inches on her.

"Or what, King, huh?" she replies.

It's the first time she's ever said my name and all I can think about is how it sounds coming from her lips.

"What are you going to do? Kidnap me? Strip me bare? Ridicule me in front of your men? Lock me up?" she sasses, throwing back everything that's happened to her over the last day. She has nothing to lose now.

"I could kill you," I point out blankly.

I get no reaction. Not a flicker of fear. Nothing.

She steps up to me so we're toe to toe.

"Dare you," she whispers.

My heart thumps harder in my chest and I can't stop my hands from twitching. I hastily wrap my fingers around her neck and push her back against the wall, pressing my body into hers. I keep replaying my name coming out of her mouth over in my head, imagining her moaning it.

Screaming it.

Theo has her head held high, extending her little neck up, allowing me more access to squeeze as she pushes into my hand. Our mouths are inches away, her hot breath tickling my lips.

"Don't tempt me, sweetheart," I say, my lips brushing hers as I speak.

She licks her lips, gently wetting mine as she does, and I bring her neck towards me before pushing her right up against the wall again, careful not to hit her head on the wall too forcefully.

Her eyes squeeze shut at the impact of the wall smashing into her back.

I'm in charge here. Let this be a reminder for her.

I let go of her neck and turn my back on her, storming past Dax and away from her cell. My dick is throbbing, begging for liberation. I burst my way into the study and grab my cock, rubbing it back and forth quickly to give myself some release. *Fuck.*

FIFTEEN MINUTES LATER, Dax walks through the door, loosening his tie and undoing his top button, whereas I discarded most of my items of clothing when I got here. My blazer is draped over the back of the chair, my tie hangs loose around my neck, my waistcoat is on the floor, and the first few buttons of my shirt are open. Relaxing into the leather chair, my feet resting up on the desk, my belt sits undone on my hips, my hat burying my face from view.

I'm swirling the dark liquid in my tumbler round and round, listening to the ice clink against the glass.

"My man," Dax says, the humour in his tone evident. "Look at you."

"Fuck off, Dax," I grunt. He laughs and sits himself down in one of the leather armchairs on the opposite side of the desk. I tilt my hat up slightly so I can see him.

"Classy." He waves his hand out in front of him, regarding my appearance, my long legs stretched out on top of the marble desk, ankles crossed. I glance down at myself and put the tumbler down to do up my belt. Dax laughs again and I groan.

"Shut the fuck up."

He holds his hands up in surrender, a hint of a smile still on his face, and I groan again, wiping my hands down my face.

"She talked a little," he says. I look up at him and drag my feet to hit the floor, sitting up straighter in the chair.

"What did she say?"

"Well, whilst you were in here jacking off, I asked her again why she killed Carlo, besides him being a dick. She said, and I quote, 'He personally hurt me. So I personally hurt him.'"

"What does that mean? How did he hurt her?" I question.

"No idea, man. She wouldn't give me much more than that. She just went quiet. Looked a little sad."

"Theodora Harlow has nothing to do with business. Her father never let her near anything important enough, so what could Carlo have done to her when she was never involved?" I know he doesn't have the answers I want, but none of this adds up. Yeah, my father wasn't a nice man, but this was personal to Theo.

Dax shakes his head in defeat. We'll have to get her to talk, but we've got plenty of time for that. I, on the other hand, need to get my shit together.

"What is it about her, man?" Dax interrupts my thoughts of Theo once again. I sigh, lifting my feet back up and putting my hat over my eyes.

"Fuck if I know."

## 8.
## Theo

The next morning when I wake, Puck is back, sitting on his stool at the entrance to my cell. I don't speak while I watch him briefly smile at me. I didn't see him again after Dax left my cell yesterday. I curled up into a ball on my mattress and didn't move until I heard the lock of the doors and then I fell asleep. But I know Puck has been sitting there ever since the doors unlocked, protecting me from all the other inmates in here.

My mind drifts back to yesterday's interruption, King's hand around my throat, slamming me against the wall. Twice.

My tongue briefly licked his lips as I licked my own. The betrayal I felt for myself, giving him any kind of intention of my desires.

It's not something I've thought about for a long time. I hate the guy. But when I saw the bulge in his trousers grow and the intensity in his eyes, his fingers wrapped around my neck, my life in his hands. It was exhilarating. I'd never felt heat like it.

But then he stormed off like a child. I thought something was happening, but clearly, I'd misunderstood. Then Dax questioned me again about Carlo. I didn't want to lie, but I didn't want to give them any more power over me. I know what I know and it's the only proof I have. They wouldn't believe me, anyway.

But Dax makes me comfortable. He isn't intimidating or rude like his cousin. They're like bad cop good cop. No wonder they are such a feared duo.

So when Dax left my cell, I curled up in a ball on my mattress and just didn't move. I thought about my innocent mother, buried in the ground. I thought about my father, who didn't even fight to protect me before King took me. Just fed me to the wolves without a goodbye.

And much to my dismay, I thought about King and his hand around my neck, his breath blowing over my lips.

Puck still has his eyes on me and my emotions are everywhere, overwhelming me. Craving some affection, I pull back the sheet and shuffle towards the wall, tapping the empty space on the mattress next to me. Puck smiles as he makes his way over and lies down, barely fitting on the mattress with me.

"Can you hold me?" I ask timidly, and with a small smile, he brings his arm up and I lift my head before laying it back down in the crook of his arm and chest.

We just lie here quietly, enjoying the company. His fingers lightly tickle my arm and his breath lightly blows over my scalp. I know it's only been a day and a half since I met him, but it feels like I've known him forever.

"What happened to your arms?" he questions, feeling the burned skin underneath his calloused fingertips. The burns on my arms don't bother me. They're growing fainter by the day, but whenever I think too much about it, it's like I can feel them burning all over again.

"My mum drowned in our bathtub and as I rushed to get to her, I knocked over a candle and set fire to the drapes. This happened whilst I was trying to put it out."

He's silent, and I think about what he said yesterday about silence giving us answers.

"It still hurts," I whisper, referring to everything, not my arms.

"It always will."

I frown at the beautiful man I'd now call my friend, listening to his heart beat softly underneath me and curiosity gets the better of me, wondering what on earth this man could've done so badly to end up here.

"Why are you in here, Puck?" I ask in a low whisper. He's silent for a while and I think he's just going to ignore the question, but then he whispers back.

"My mother was one of Carlo Rhivers' housemaids. When I was sixteen, my father was killed, caught up accidentally in a shooting happening between the Districts and some outsiders from the Newlands. So I was sent to live with my ma at the Rhivers' mansion."

I frown at his confession, mourning his father with him.

"You'd have loved my ma. She made the best mac and cheese."

I laugh and his chuckle vibrates through his chest.

"What's her name?" I ask.

"Maria. God, I wish I knew if she's still alive. I haven't seen King or Dax in so long, I haven't been able to ask them."

My gut churns and I hope one day he can find the answers he's looking for.

"You're close with King and Dax?"

"I was, once."

I think about his story but still don't really know why he's here.

"Puck, I still don't understand."

He sighs, pain laced with his voice. "Whilst walking around the grounds one day, I met the most beautiful girl. You can call me naïve, but we fell in love. Two years later, I got her pregnant."

I furrow my brow.

"It was his daughter."

I shoot my head up, looking at Puck to make sense of what he's saying.

"Whose daughter?"

"Carlo's," Puck says so quietly.

"Carlo has a daughter?" I'm trying to think of any recollection of knowledge about Carlo having a daughter. *King has a sister?*

"Carlo *had* a daughter," he continues to whisper, emphasising the past tense. "A year younger than King. He hid her away, convinced she wasn't his. He could *never have had a girl.*" Puck imitates a childlike voice. "No one knew about her apart from those in the Rhivers' mansion circle." He pauses again, collecting his thoughts. "I was eighteen and she was sixteen when she fell pregnant. Carlo sent me straight here."

I feel his heart beat faster, knowing what's coming next.

"What happened to her?" I ask quietly, laying my head back on his chest.

"He killed her. And my baby." His voice cracks and my eyes water. She was hidden all her life, only to fall in love and die for it. I take a deep breath and hold on to his shirt.

"And what was her name?" I ask, so I can pray for her and her baby to be at peace.

"Bonnie." There's a smile in his voice as he says her name.

I smile, picturing Puck with his Bonnie.

After a few moments of silence, I look up at him. He holds me and my hand leaves his chest to hold his cheek. I lean in, gently brushing my lips against his, but quickly pull back.

He looks into my eyes briefly before putting his hand onto my cheek and bringing my head back in. He passionately kisses me as I kiss him back.

It's not heated or giving me a fluttering feeling in the pit of my stomach, but it's comforting. I know his heart lies with the memory of his young love, his baby's mother, and after the confusing emotions around King, this just feels right to explore.

The whistle announcing shower time interrupts us and he winks at me, the cheerful Puck back. He grabs my hand, pulling me up with him as he leads us to the showers again.

ONCE IN THE SHOWER BLOCK, we stick to the same routine as yesterday, except I let Puck go first so I don't use his towel again. I stand facing the wall to avoid looking at anything that will make me heave, excluding Puck, but thinking about the bulge I saw growing in King's pants yesterday, I start to squirm.

I roll my head from shoulder to shoulder to try and clear

the thought of Puck standing there without his trousers on. Curiosity gets the better of me and I turn my head slightly to take a peek at Puck as he showers. He washes his face under the spray and my eyes travel lower over his rock-hard abs before landing between his legs.

I'm not attracted to Puck like that, but looking at a naked man is just bringing inappropriate thoughts of King. Would his body look like this? Ripped and muscled? Would he be *that* big?

After staring for way too long, I notice how still Puck's standing and my eyes dart back to his face. He's smiling at me, an eyebrow raised in amusement.

"Like what you see?" He winks.

I blush and smile before turning back to the wall. God, I can't believe I just got caught. Small flutters of butterflies fly rapidly in my stomach at the embarrassment.

Once the shower stops, he dries himself off and ties the towel around his waist. He grabs mine off the hook and makes the same barrier as he did for me yesterday.

I take off my jumpsuit and turn the water on, then place myself under the spray, a little used to the coldness now. A crazy thought runs through my mind as I look at Puck's lean back before tapping him on the shoulder. He turns his head slightly, pinning his eyes right on mine.

"It's only fair right?" I smile, opening my arms. Puck laughs before shrugging his shoulders and changing his position to face me. I'm not sure where the sudden burst of confidence came from, but it's not like that between us. Besides, the attention feels nice.

So I shower under his watchful gaze, conscious of my scarred arms but not afraid to hide them, watching him follow my hands as I wash myself. Every now and then, we both laugh with each other at the ridiculous situation we've found ourselves in.

"Well, if you'd told me I'd be doing this a week ago..." He winks as I swat him on the arm. I have no idea what I'm doing, but it feels right. I don't think of Puck the way I think of King and he doesn't make me feel the way King made me feel yesterday, but he's the closest thing I've got and I'm keeping it that way.

## 9. King

I couldn't seem to leave the prison. Knowing she was in there, alone and partly vulnerable, kept me here. A sadistic part of me was turned on by the thoughts of her fear and panic but another part of me worried that I'd left her here in the first place. She has wedged herself into my mind and won't budge. She's slowly becoming an obsession.

Dax keeps protesting about having to stay and work, wanting to get back home, but I can't find it in me to leave. The Districts fall on me now that Carlo's dead. I can't run it from inside these walls no matter how much I want to.

It's midnight and I'm just wrapping it up, convincing myself to leave because she's locked in her cell now anyway, when Dax comes through the door, silently collecting his coat.

"Are you ready to go?" I ask, knowing he is as he's been waiting for me for the last few hours.

"Yeah, all good," he says, shrugging his arms into his coat. "I heard our new little prisoner put on a little show in the showers today." He says it casually, fixing his collar.

I freeze on the spot, with only one arm in my blazer, and if looks could kill, Dax would be on the ground.

"Excuse me?" I question, the anger boiling up to the surface at the thought of all of the lowlifes in there watching Theo shower, getting to enjoy a front row seat to her curved body and round breasts, all wet and soapy.

"Easy, cuz, Puck was holding the towel around her again. He was just facing her. Guards said he was watching her the whole time she showered, both of them laughing together." Dax thinks he's settling my anger by reassuring me it was in fact Puck with that front row seat, but he's only intensifying it.

"That little prick," I spit, shrugging my blazer back off my arm and storming for the door.

"King, leave it. What's it to you?" Dax protests at my tantrum.

"Wait for me," I shout as I leave the room. Dax sighs loudly at my retreating back.

My blood boils as I think of Puck's eyes trailing all over Theo's body. When I asked him to keep an eye on her, I didn't mean *literally*.

I slam my way through doors, trying not to make too much noise but not having the restraint to be quiet as I make my way to Theo's cell. I glance into Puck's as I pass, seeing him asleep on his mattress, and I ball my hands into fists.

I'll deal with him tomorrow.

I stand against Theo's cell, gripping tightly onto the bars, and to my surprise, her soft eyes find mine.

She's sat up on her mattress, legs crossed, just quietly staring into the dark.

It's like she was waiting for me. Like she knew I'd come.

I'm caught between worrying about why she isn't asleep and wanting to yank her hair back and punish her for letting

Puck watch something so intimate. Something that should've been mine.

Slowly standing up, never taking her eyes off mine, she saunters over to me and stands almost up against the bars and all over again I'm fuming that I left the keys in the study so there's no way of me getting to her. I didn't think this through. She crosses her arms over her chest as she stares me down.

"What do you want, King?" she whispers.

I grind my teeth together at the sight of her buried under her jumpsuit. I haven't been able to get her body out of my mind since I stripped her, and now someone else has seen her with fresh eyes, so I say the only logical thing that comes to mind.

"Strip," I reply quietly, déjà vu from a couple days ago resurfacing. She laughs at me, walking closer to the bars. She's just a breath away and I could reach out and grab her if I wanted to. And fuck do I want to.

"Can't handle another man's eyes on me, King?" she teases, connecting the dots as to why I'm here. The more she says my name, the harder my dick gets.

"You don't need another man's eyes on you, sweetheart," I growl, seeing her squirm slightly.

"I liked it," she admits, shrugging her shoulders with a ghost of a smile before turning away.

But I'm quicker.

I grab her arm and slam her back against the bars. A loud echoing sound fills the prison, but I'm done caring.

My hand finds her throat, my palm now familiar with the position as Theo's back presses up against the bars and as much of me as I can fit through them. She extends her neck again, giving me more access to splay my fingers around her throat.

Her pulse quickens, her breath stutters, and I don't miss the tip of her tongue peeking out to wet her lips. I flex my fingers on her neck, loving the feel of her at my complete mercy and through the bars, I look down at her hidden body and the urge to have her naked again wins out.

She doesn't fight me as my other hand moves up her side, over her breast as I grab hold of the zipper at the top of her jumpsuit.

"You liked it, did you?" I murmur, as I slowly pull it down, exposing her skin, the descent of the zipper loud in the silence.

"Mhmm," she mumbles, watching what I'm doing.

"Did you want him to touch you?" I whisper in her ear as the zipper hits the end at her crotch and there's nowhere else for it to go. Her body is completely exposed to me, her breasts round and her nipples hard. I can't see much further down because of the bars between us, but I can remember what her pussy looked like. I'll never forget it.

"Yes," she whispers to my question. I know she isn't thinking about Puck now, but I can't help but play into the fantasy.

"Did you want him to touch you like this?" I ask as I glide a finger around the curve of her breast and lightly over her nipple, following the actions with the other. She breathes heavily, her nipples pebbling further, and her stomach sucks in on a small gasp as my finger travels lower.

I slowly slide in between her folds, my finger instantly feeling the warmth and wetness that's coating her between her legs. She moans as my finger spreads her wetness around, rubbing over her clit in soft circles.

"He can't touch you like I can, sweetheart," I whisper into her ear.

After a few more strokes of her clit, I pull my hand away from her heat and hold it out in front of her, my finger glistening with her.

"Take off my rings."

She hesitates a moment and I tighten the hand clamped around her neck. She whimpers and then her hands find mine and she slowly, one by one, pulls my rings off my fingers and holds them tightly in a fist.

I return my hand back between her legs and continue teasing her. Slowly, my fingers travel lower, my thumb still playing with her clit, whilst my middle finger rests impatiently at her entrance.

"Who can touch you like this? Like I can?" I whisper again, speeding up my thumb, flicking her nub as her breathing quickens. I tighten my hand around her neck again at her lack of response.

"Who can touch you like I can, Theodora?" I growl.

"No one," she breathes out so quietly, that if I wasn't listening, I would've probably missed it.

"Good girl."

I push my finger into her entrance and she's so wet, I slide in easily, right to the knuckle before moving it back out. I push back into her with two fingers, going as deep as I can, satisfied that I made her take off my rings. Her back arches, but her ass and head are still pressed up against the bars.

She moans as my fingers quicken, hitting her deeper with

every thrust, her moans and wetness deafening in the quiet space.

"Quiet now, sweetheart, or you'll give everyone a show."

She bites her lip in an attempt to stifle her moans, but it doesn't do much. She looks and feels so goddamn sexy, and I'm furious the bars are restricting me from having all of her in my hands. I can feel her pussy clenching around my fingers as her breathing spirals out of control.

"Say my name, sweetheart," I demand, waiting to finally hear her moan on my name. "Say my name when you come on my fingers."

Her knees buckle and her hips jerk. She's held up solely by my hand around her neck that tightens even more as she moans my name breathlessly, filling the silent walls of the prison with my goddamn fucking name whilst she comes undone.

"King!"

To hear my name from her lips again unleashes a feral need within me. To finally have her crumbling at my mercy after so many years is euphoric. And if Theo wasn't occupying my every waking thought before, she certainly is now. I'll never be able to unhear the way she just said my name. *Never.* And I'll be damned if it's the last time I do.

I slow my fingers as she comes down from her high, her legs finding some strength to stand up on her own, and I pull my fingers out and quickly swipe one last time over her clit, making her quiver.

I travel my hand up to her chest and over each nipple, trailing her wetness over each pebbled bud whilst she catches her breath. With difficulty, I release her neck and she turns around so I can see her in all her glory.

Her pussy is weeping, her nipples are rock-solid, and they're glistening with her cum. The red fingerprint marks around her neck make a beautiful accessory I'd love to see on her every day.

She looks lazily up at me, biting down on her bottom lip, watching intently as I bring my fingers up to my mouth, still wet from her, and suck on them. The heat in her eyes intensifies as I taste her on my tongue.

I reach my hand out once more, grabbing her waist and snaking my arm around her back, pressing her into the metal bars. Her flesh hugs the bars, each breast sticking out in between, an invitation if I ever saw one. She hisses at the cold but softly moans as I flick her nipple with my tongue.

"Next time," I say normally, not worried about keeping quiet anymore so she can hear the seriousness in my voice, "I'm tasting you."

She licks her lips, about to speak before I interrupt her again.

"Put on a shower show for anyone again and I'll make you regret it."

I release her and walk away, disappearing out the door before I find myself turning around and breaking into her cell.

Now that I've felt her come undone on my fingers and briefly tasted her on my tongue, I'm not sure how I'll ever leave this goddamn prison.

# 10.
# Theo

I've been in this cell for a total of three days, roughly seventy-two hours stuck confined within the same four walls. I miss the daylight and fresh air, the sun beaming down, burning my skin until it's a glowing tan, strays of my hair sticking to my neck as sweat beads coat the top layer of my body all over.

I even miss the rain that freezes my pores, soaks my clothing, and mats my hair. The thrill of walking under the raindrops, rinsing away your sorrows.

But the simple pleasures of Mother Nature are robbed from you in here. There's no sun. There's no rain. There's just damp and cold and terribly unnatural dim lighting.

I've felt like a prisoner for most of my life. My father never gave me the privileges most teenage daughters had, like getting to go out with their friends, meet boys, have parties. Even the simple pleasure of going to school daily, something I know most teenagers complain about. But what wouldn't I have done to go to school even for a day.

I've been home-schooled all my life. My only friends were my mother and Emerson, who technically doesn't count considering my father paid him to watch over me.

There was only one other friend I really treasured closely, but he disappeared as quickly as he came.

So feeling secluded, trapped, and like a prisoner isn't new to me.

But no amount of exclusion or depravity from normal life would've compared to this. What I wouldn't give to be stuck at my father's mansion, at least with the freedom to roam the outdoors and the grounds without having to watch my back.

At least this place has given me Puck.

At the thought of him, I turn on my mattress and look over to where I find him every morning, sitting on his stool in his usual place.

Except he's not there.

My eyes scan my cell in one swift motion, wondering if I've woken up before the doors open, but then I notice other inmates walking and talking beyond my closed gate. Where is he?

I shift to a sitting position and a fire pools low in my belly and I squirm, the reminder of last night creeping up my skin. I remember King's hands on me, his fingers in me, and I clench my thighs together.

I've been sexual before with Emerson, only some basic foreplay and sex, but that was only once and a few years ago now. A rebellious moment where I was angry at my father and wanted to get back at him in some secret way.

I also wanted to lose my virginity before it was either stolen from me or it would never happen. But nothing with Emerson felt as intimate and electrifying as last night with King. And all he did was use his fingers.

I suddenly feel like a blossoming teenager with her first crush and having no idea what to do.

It's pathetic.

What was King doing? Why did he come here last night? Am I being easy? Is he interested or is he stringing me along... again?

A million questions rack my brain and I wish my mum were here to talk about it.

Puck will have to do for now.

I stand up on slightly shaky legs and head over to the gate to make my way to Puck's cell where he must still be asleep or knowing him, doing some kind of workout. Before stepping out of the safety of my cell, I call his name just to double-check, but as his name leaves my lips, a tall, slim man, who is most definitely not Puck, walks out of his cell and stands in front of me, the gate my only protection remaining between us.

My hands tighten around the bars as the stranger watches me. He cocks his head and smiles, licking his lips, and a shiver escapes down my spine, fear creeping in.

How can so much change in a few hours? These bars last night were a hindrance, an inconvenience, locked when we wanted them open to give us more access to each other.

Whereas now they're all I have for safety and the damn thing is unlocked.

"Puck," I call out again a little louder, my voice shaking, waiting for him to appear from his cell and offer me the protection I've become so accustomed to.

"Puck's not here, sweetheart."

I almost heave at the nickname, hating how it sounds

from his lips, the opposite effect it has on me when King uses it.

The man brushes a greasy strand of hair out of his eyes and steps closer, placing his hands on the bars above mine. I immediately tighten my grip, pushing all my force into keeping the bars closed, but I'm not strong enough against him and the gate slides open, my safety net gone.

I stagger backwards to the opposite wall to create as much distance as I can between us. I know I've been extremely lucky having Puck in my corner, but I've clearly taken his protection for granted considering the first time I'm left alone without him, I'm vulnerable, with no idea how to protect myself.

Sure, I could put up a good fight, but that isn't going to last me in the long run. Not with that gate wide-open, easily accessible to every sleaze in here.

The guy approaches me in a few steps and towers over me easily, like all men in my life seem to do.

He reaches out a dirty hand and strokes my cheek with the back of his knuckles and I cringe, turning my head away, trying to get away from his touch.

I tense my jaw, suck in my cheeks, and spit in his face, adrenaline coursing through my veins.

The only option I have left is to fight back.

I lift my fist to hit him right across the cheek, but the momentum behind it does nothing to help me as he grips my wrist just as I make contact. He yanks it above my head and pins it up against the wall, grabbing my other wrist harshly and joining my hands together. I kick and try to wriggle myself free, but it's no use. He's too strong. I try my hardest not to scream, not to cause a scene and lure in any more unwanted guests. I'm screaming inside, praying with all I have that this isn't real.

"Keep still, bitch," he spits, striking a hand across my face, the sting kicking in immediately, "or it's gonna be a lot more painful."

The spray of his saliva coats my skin and my eyes well up from the slap and the situation I've found myself in. His free hand finds the zipper to his jumpsuit as he pulls it down, releasing his erection, and I try to hold back my bile. He smirks again as his hand finds the zipper to my own jumpsuit, pulling it all the way down, baring my naked chest and way below my thighs, the large jumpsuit sagging at my knees.

His hand slides over my helpless body, grabbing harshly at my breasts and pulling tightly on my nipples and ever so slowly, his hand slips lower between my thighs, cupping my mound, and tears slip silently from my eyes.

# 11. King

Puck sits under the dim light, his hands tied up behind his back, blood pouring out of his nose from the fresh set of punches I gave him moments ago. My knuckles crack from the blow, but my fist stays clenched.

After visiting Theo's cell last night, I can't get her out of my head. How it felt to have her under my hands, hearing my name escape her lips, how her body looked, glistening in her cum as she stood naked and exposed in front of me. But my blood boils when I think of Puck staring at the same curves, admiring her peachy ass in the showers that same day.

Did he notice the small freckle that hides just under her left breast? Or the faint scars that burden her arms? Did he see the pink of her pussy, her pebbled nipples?

I'm hungry for Theo, but I'm thirsty for blood. And unfortunately for Puck, it's his.

"What the fuck is this, man?" Puck spits, a clot of blood landing on the floor at my feet. He has the audacity to sound confused as to why I dragged him to the interrogation room before doors opened this morning.

The room is empty aside from the single chair Puck is

tied to and the shitty lightbulb on the ceiling that's so dim, it might as well not work. There's a mirror on one wall that's two-way, like all good interrogation rooms have, and I know Dax is standing on the other side. Probably shaking his head at my sudden change in behaviour.

He's fed up with me and he's fed up with spending so much time here, but I can't seem to do business elsewhere. My father's funeral is looming over our heads and the entire empire of the First District is still waiting for me to properly take the reins, but this goddamn prison is all I can think about. I rear my fist back for another round when Puck shouts at me before I take my swing.

"King, what the fuck!"

I hesitate and look at him, seeing the genuine confusion in his eyes.

"I'll take a beating, you know I will, but tell me what the fuck it is I did first."

I lower my fist and lean closer so we're eye to eye.

"You know what you did, Puck."

He just glares at me, which only winds me up even more. "Please, enlighten me."

I glance over at the mirror, looking at Dax through my reflection, then turn my head back to Puck.

"You fucking look at or touch Theodora again, I swear to God I will slit your throat right here," I say, baring my teeth at him.

He halts for a minute. A sudden look of surprise, then a smile shadows over his face before a full belly laugh erupts from his mouth.

*What the fuck?*

My anger resurfaces and I clench my fist again, ramming

it into the side of his jaw so he chokes on his laugh at the blow of the punch.

"Okay, okay," he says, spitting out some more blood.

"The fuck you laughing at, Puck? You think this is amusing?"

He shakes his head, the smile ghosting his features again.

"I think it's amusing that you've actually dragged my ass in here to beat the shit out of me over jealousy for the girl. Are you kidding me?"

"I'm not fucking jealous," I spit but lower my hand in defeat.

"You got a crush on the girl, King? Hey, didn't she kill your dad like three days ago?" He chuckles again.

"You have some nerve laughing about this, Pucker." His old nickname rolls off my tongue like in the old days.

"You've got some nerve tying me up and beating the shit out of me over this, *King*. Untie my fucking hands, mate."

I sigh and untie his hands from the ropes, and he rubs them both in his hands, easing his wrists as Dax enters the room smiling, giving Puck a handshake.

"What the fuck's gotten into him?" Puck says to Dax, pointing to me over his shoulder.

"Kid's losing it, mate. I haven't been able to get him to leave the prison since she walked through the doors. Hell, she's fucking walking all over him. If I didn't know him better, I'd say he was in love with the girl," Dax retaliates, encouraging him. Both of them laugh and it takes everything in me not to shoot them here and now.

"Fuck off, he isn't!" Puck says through his laughter.

"No, I'm not fucking in love with her, but I swear if you touch her again, I will kill you, Puck."

After composing himself, Puck tucks his smile away and turns to face me head-on.

"Calm down, bro, nothing's happening with me and T. Like I'd get caught between whatever fucking game you've got going on."

T? So she's got a fucking nickname now.

"What was the shower situation yesterday then?" I respond, my blood starting to reheat at the thought of Puck seeing her naked body.

"It was a bit of a laugh. She saw my dick, so she repaid the favour," he says calmly, shrugging his shoulders.

"She saw your dick?" I shout, ready to cut his dick off.

"Look, I know we can't all be as big as me, but she'll get over it." He winks.

He fucking winks.

I start towards him before he advances on me and pushes me up against the wall, his arm against my throat.

"King. You know I don't give a shit about other women. I had Bonnie. So fucking get over yourself. I'm looking out for her. Protecting her. Like *you* asked me to do. So put the green monster away and pull yourself together."

He lets go of me and I look down to fix my collar and tie. The mention of Bonnie clouds my vision and thoughts of my little sister haunt my conscience.

"I love Bonnie, King. I'll only ever love Bonnie like that and you've spent enough time with me in and out of this shit hole to know that."

I nod, knowing he's telling the truth. The pain that follows both of us from Bonnie's name and our time together in this prison lingers in the air and I clear my throat.

"Sorry, man." He nods and pats me on the back.

"Get me a fucking towel, would ya." He chuckles, gesturing to his bloody nose.

---

The three of us leave the interrogation room and head back towards the cells, and the noise grows from silence to murmurs to full conversations as we enter the main cell block. The inmates are walking around, entering and leaving each other's cells, and a slice of dread hits me like a ton of bricks as my eyes scan up to the first floor and notice Theo's cell wide-open.

"Fuck." I start to run, Dax and Puck right on my tail. I got Puck out of his cell to interrogate him before the gates opened so he could be back for Theo when they did, but I must've lost track of time.

Anger makes its way up to the surface at the possibility that something has happened to Theo, left unprotected in a prison full of men, all because of me.

As we climb the stairs, I jump over the top railing and my feet land firmly in front of Theo's cell. I find her instantly and her eyes lock with mine, panic and fear glistening in her blue orbs, tears falling slowly and silently.

Her jumpsuit is zipped open down to her knees, like it was for me last night, except this time, the hand of some sleazy criminal cups her pussy whilst restraining her, his lips latched onto her neck.

I barge straight in, not wasting any time, and grab the back of his jumpsuit, ripping him off of Theo and slamming him against the wall.

His jumpsuit, also undone, sags against his thin frame, his limp dick flopping at the sight of me. He starts to protest when he realises who's interrupted him and the sweet smell of fear emanates from him.

Dax holds him up against the wall, repeatedly swinging his fist into the criminal whilst Puck assists in holding him up for Dax to take more blows. I turn to Theo, who is frozen in place, watching the scene unfold. I rake my eyes down her body, looking for any bruises or harm that could've come to her.

Approaching her slowly, her eyes find mine again and the fear has now disappeared and is replaced with something else. I pull the zipper of her jumpsuit all the way up, covering her modesty, and cup her face in my hands, wiping her remaining tears with my thumbs.

She grabs a fistful of the jumpsuit in her hands and wipes where his mouth was on her neck moments ago. I pull her hands away and kiss her in the exact same spot, gently licking at her skin to replace the feel of the sleazebag and leaving her with only traces of me.

I'll have to do the same for her pussy later.

Bringing my head back up, level with hers, I stare intently into her eyes, hers completely void of tears now.

"Did he hurt you?" I can see she's really thinking my question through until she shakes her head slowly.

"Where did he touch you? Did his dick touch you?"

She shakes her head again. "Just his hand," she whispers almost inaudibly.

"It's not *just* anything, Theodora," I whisper back. I turn to look over my shoulder to face Dax and Puck, who have the prick held up against the wall.

"W-what you expect, man? There are no rules here. Of course I wanted some of that."

I raise my brows at the balls of this guy to not only call me *man* but assume that it's okay to fucking talk to me in the first place, especially about raping women.

"Yeah, *man*? Well, I want some of you."

His eyebrows furrow as he replays what I said.

I reach behind my blazer and pull the gun from my holster, holding it up directly in front of his head.

"There's nothing sweeter than blood," I taunt, as I pull the trigger and the bullet disappears right through his skull. Theo flinches behind me and blood splatters all over us and the walls, coating us in crimson paint.

Everyone's silent for several seconds before a shout interrupts the peace that's haunting us all.

"Shower time."

I tense, staring around at all of us, no one showing any sign of moving, almost as still as the dead man at our feet. There's no way in hell I'm having Theo shower with them all now, even with Puck watching over her. I grab her hand and lead her towards the open doorway to her cell.

"Theo," a small voice says, breaking our bubble of silence, and Theo halts and we both turn to the voice. Puck looks at her with an overwhelming sadness, drops of blood coating his face all over.

"I'm sorry," he says.

Theo gives him a small smile, a peace offering, an act of forgiveness.

"It wasn't your fault," she says before turning on her heel, gripping tighter onto my hand and letting me lead her away.

## 12.
## Theo

King's grip on my hand is tight, but I squeeze his right back, in fear of him letting me go, in fear of being the prey for all of these predators again. I have no idea what I was expecting, being surrounded by men who've been locked up from the outside world, but I should've expected it eventually. I'd grown accustomed to Puck's protection and the denial that although he sent me here, King wouldn't actually let me get hurt.

How naive I've become in the span of three days.

Puck's been my hero, my protector, but could I really have expected him to be there for me every second of every day? King hasn't really given me any indication that I'll be safe, but I still thought I would be.

But neither of them was there and I can't really blame them for it. But where was Puck in the first place? And he came back with King and Dax... Why were they all together? Through the trauma, I think about Puck. Wasn't his nose bleeding? What happened?

I look down at the hand that's casing mine, his skin hidden beneath black tattoos, and his fingers are long, meeting each other as they wrap around my small hand. But on top of the ink and muscle, his knuckles are cracked and bloody. What happened between them?

My thoughts continue to drift off at a thousand miles an hour when I realise my legs are still carrying me forward, following my enemy. Is he still that? My enemy?

The noise of the prison is gone, replaced by my quick breaths at trying to keep up with King, being practically dragged through dark corridors. We stop at a door and King takes out a key from his pocket, never letting go of my hand.

He unlocks the abandoned door at the dead end of the corridor and forces it open, pulling me inside behind him.

King lets go of my hand as he turns to lock the door we just came through, but I'm stuck in a trance, mesmerised by the bright sunlight soaking through the large floor-to-ceiling window on the opposite wall.

My feet carry me over to it of their own accord and I place my palms flat against the cool glass, scanning the view, taking in the sight of the forested area in front of me, thick tree trunks and bright green leaves, a blue sky completing the postcard picture.

I rest my forehead in between my palms and a tear slips down my cheek.

"It's beautiful," I whisper, more to myself.

"It's just trees," King's deep voice replies, right behind me. I jump a little at the proximity and turn my head over my shoulder to peek at him, my hands never leaving the glass.

"*Just trees* is a damn right better sight than those four walls I have to look at every day." I turn my head back to the window. "You wouldn't understand."

My breath fogs up the window in front of me.

King leans into me and his hand reaches from under my arm, one ringed finger writing *I do* in the fog on the window before it disappears forever. We stand there for a beat, bodies pressed against each other, the rise and fall of my chest growing rapidly the longer we're stuck here.

"You've been in here before." I break the silence, a statement more than a question. King reacts instantly, stiffening, and steps away from me, the moment gone.

"You need to shower," he says and walks off to the left, disappearing through a doorway. I look down at myself, at the red splattering of blood covering the grey jumpsuit, and my mind flickers back again to the scene we just left. A dead man who had just assaulted me, on the floor of my cell, by the hand of King Rhivers. No remorse, no hesitation.

All to protect me.

I hear a door slam and I'm jerked out of my thoughts once more. I assume I'm supposed to follow, so I drag myself away from the window and head through the same door King disappeared through.

I find myself in a bathroom bigger than my cell, his and hers sinks that are completely empty of possessions, not even a toothbrush in sight.

King stands next to a large walk-in shower, the water already running, steam rising into the air vents above. The water looks heavenly and I shuffle on my feet, itching to get under it.

King uncrosses his arms and gestures towards the shower with his right hand, giving me permission to go ahead. I walk straight under the water, not even bothering to remove my jumpsuit, desperate to feel the water burn my skin, and I marvel at the feeling, relaxing into the sensation.

I fumble for the zipper on my jumpsuit and pull it down, quickly stepping out of it to feel the full force of the water on my body. The spray is powerful, beating down on my flesh, cleansing me.

Minutes must pass before I remember where I am—and that I'm not alone. I turn my head from the shower, water droplets dripping from my eyelashes, my vision still slightly blurred, and King is watching me, leaning against the glass, looking right into my eyes, no sign of hesitation or surrender to take his gaze down my body. Not that he hasn't had more than an eyeful before, but he's respectful now.

"Wash him away, sweetheart," he says, his deep, low voice awakening something inside me. I turn away from him to grab the soap from the shelf. Compared to the small, grimy bar of soap in the communal showers, this one is a bright white and smells heavenly.

Between my palms, I lather up as much soap as I can, then face King, rubbing my hands over my arms and shoulders, back and forth before lowering to my breasts. I knead them in slow circles, the bubbles from the soap sticking to my skin.

King's eyes follow my hands everywhere they go. Up each arm, over the shoulder, then down to circle each breast, slowly. I pinch my nipple between my fingers, biting my lip to try and stifle any moans that want to escape. It's not the feeling that's overtaking me when I touch myself that makes me want to cry out but the way King's ogling me.

I slowly pass my hands over my stomach, descending lower until I reach the heat between my legs. I slide one finger between my folds and feel the wetness that has gathered there, and not from the shower.

A moment of doubt creeps into my mind when I think about what happened to me only moments ago and how already I'm willing to touch myself, but then King's words echo in my head

*Wash him away, sweetheart.*

King watches me hungrily as I play with myself but shows no sign of joining me and despite myself, I want him to.

I stop what I'm doing and slowly make my way over to King. He doesn't take his gaze off me and it strikes me how intimidated he makes me feel and I wonder where this sudden burst of confidence has come from.

I reach out and take his hand in mine, turning it over and rubbing my thumb over the cracked bloody knuckles. He doesn't wince or pull away, his eyes burning a hole right through me.

I pull him towards me as I make my way back into the shower. He doesn't resist, which is the only reassurance I need.

I pull us both under the shower head, water pelting down on my naked skin and the layers of material through his suit. I rub his knuckles back and forth under the water until all the blood is gone, then bring his hand up to my lips and gently kiss them, softly lapping my tongue over the cracks. I pull my head up and look at him.

His shirt is soaked through, his blazer hanging heavily on his shoulders. King grabs my arms, pulling me closer. His calloused fingers rub up and down each arm, twirling around the scarring as he looks at them closely for the first time.

"What happened?" he asks softly.

He frowns at my scars, like he's pained to see the history

of what happened etched onto my skin. I clear my throat and look down at them myself.

"I found my mother in the bath when she, when she…" I clear my throat, trying to get the words out after having only relived this moment already with Puck recently. "Anyway, there was a candle on the sink and I knocked it off in my panic. It set fire to the drapes and I tried to pull them down to put it out. I was lucky, though."

He looks up at me, but I still watch his fingers following the scars on my arms.

"I jumped in the bath, so the water soothed it, stopped it from scarring too badly. Over the past two years, they've healed well. They're barely there."

My voice cracks as I finish my sentence. The pain of that night comes back to me. Every day I think of my scars healing is just another reminder that life's moving on whether I want it to or not.

"I don't want them to heal," I whisper. "This is all I have left of her."

I know how that must sound, but these scars are the only visible reminder of that night. The proof of my pain, the proof of my loss. Without them, what if I forget what all of this was for?

"The scars that heal on the outside will never fully heal on the inside, Theodora. The scars on your heart, that's what you'll have left."

I look into his eyes, mine glistening with tears, and he gently cups my cheek.

"I'm sorry you lost your mother, Theodora."

"I'm sorry you lost yours, too."

My words take him by surprise and he studies my face,

flicking from my eyes to my lips, and in one swift movement, he leans in and his lips crash against mine, a burst of passion shooting from my lips down to my toes. I wrap my arms around his neck, reaching up on my tiptoes to bring us closer.

He lifts me easily and I wrap my legs around him, our lips never breaking. My tongue dances with his as I tangle my hands in his hair, pulling at the collar of his shirt, a hunger in me, desperate for more.

The shower continues to pour as he stands there with me in his arms, both of us pulling away at the same time. Our eyes frantically find each other like our mouths did, the hunger just as obvious in him as it is in me. We catch our breath and I lean back in, desperate for more, and King doesn't hesitate, kissing me right back.

He takes a few steps forward, my back hitting the shower wall, and I drop my legs and start to pull off his blazer, annoyed at the lack of skin he's giving me. He lets me pull it off before coming back in for more, his mouth finding mine, cupping my jaw, whilst his other hand starts to travel lower.

His fingers tickle my lower belly, my thigh, my hip. Everywhere but *there* and I whimper at the need for his touch. He smiles through the kiss and his finger finally hits that sweet spot, relieving me of some of the pent-up pressure.

King bites my lip gently before pulling away and lowering himself to kiss my chest, my nipples, my stomach, landing on my inner thigh. He's on both knees, looking up at me, and it's the most beautiful sight I've ever seen.

"I told you next time I'd taste you," he says, breaking the silence. His tongue laps me up from bottom to top and my knees instantly buckle. His hands pin me to the wall at my hips to keep me upright whilst his tongue continuously licks my clit in slow, tantalising strokes. Fire starts to burn low in my stomach as King's tongue works faster.

"Say my name, sweetheart," King says from between my legs and the sound of his voice instantly sends shooting sensations up through my core. I moan his name, over and over, loving the sound of it on my lips.

"King. King. King."

King keeps up the pace, devouring me, switching his tongue from torturous flicks to my clit, to diving it deep into my pussy, lapping my juices from me. The tension builds and I arch my back, my hands pulling tightly at King's hair, and my orgasm reaches its peak.

"That's it, Theodora, now be a good girl and come for me."

Following his command, my body rides out an orgasm, so powerful and strong, like champagne bubbles bursting from the cork. I continue to ride my high as long as King's tongue continues to tease my clit until my legs give up and King lets go of my hips, gently bringing me to the floor with him. He kisses me roughly, the taste of me all over him turning me on more.

My hands find his hair again, tugging at him to pull him as close to me as possible.

I feel completely vulnerable, caught in a moment of weakness, but King's giving me everything back. This isn't rough and rushed like last night. This is passionate and slow, and I'm craving more and more of him.

His mouth claims mine, and for a brief second, I remember the feel of his lips, the taste of his tongue and how familiar his kiss is and a small whimper leaves me, overwhelmed by what's happened and how we ended up here.

King pulls away to look at me, and the ecstasy of the last few minutes dissipates when my eyes find his, cold and bored. With a quick shuffle, King manoeuvres himself to standing and looks down at me, really looks down at me, like a peasant, spent and breathless on the floor.

"Clean up, sweetheart," he says bluntly before turning and walking away from me without a look back.

His blazer lies in a sopping puddle on the floor of the shower, along with me.

# 13. King

I peel off the remaining items of my wet clothing, throw them to the floor with a wet slap, and wrap a towel around my waist. Leaning up against the wall-length window, my palm leaves a wet outline, the condensation rippling under my breath.

My dick is still rock-hard, the taste of Theo still lingering on my tongue, and I groan in defeat. I should have never let this happen. This girl murdered my father. I can't be entirely angry over the fact she killed him, but I'm angry that she beat me to it.

I can't let this get to me anymore. I have the goddamn Districts to run. Everything now falls on my shoulders and if I don't get my head out of this fog when I'm around Theo, I'll fuck up everything I've been training my whole life for.

I just need to fucking get over Theo. Or fuck her to get her out of my system, then I can move on and forget this ridiculousness.

Yeah, that's what I'll do.

I stalk back into the bathroom, hasty and forceful, and my predatory eyes fall on Theo's naked backside as she stands under the spray. I fling my towel to the floor, my dick finally springing free and Theo turns at the sound of the heavy thud slapping onto the wet floor.

Her eyes are wide, first looking at my steel rod erection for a beat too long before settling them on mine. As if sensing the shift in me, she takes a step back until she's backed up against the wall. Her breaths are coming quicker, her chest heavily rising and falling at rapid speed as I approach her. She looks frightened, but there's something else there too. Arousal maybe?

In a few more strides, I'm within reaching distance and I snake my arm around her waist, pulling her flush against me. She gasps at the movement and a smirk appears across my face. I like that noise coming from her pretty little lips.

I bite down on her bottom lip hard to hear her whimper like that again. She moans quietly, almost like she's trying to withhold her pleasure.

Her hands grip my biceps firmly and I'm readying to lift her straight onto my cock, but she pushes me backwards and the surprise shocks me enough that my arm loosens from around her slim frame. Her eyes have turned from searing heat to a glaze of disgust, her arousal clearly diminished.

She reaches up to stroke her lip, wiping away the bead of blood that rose to the surface, my teeth marks visible on the inside of her lower lip. My cock gets harder, if that's even possible, seeing my imprint on her.

Theo, however, doesn't seem to be on the same wavelength as me and my anger starts to boil its way up to the surface yet again. I don't know what she does to me, but anger is an emotion that constantly surrounds me when it comes to Theodora Harlow. Memories from before lit the flame and moments now keep it burning. I'm a constant fire ignited with gasoline whenever I'm around her.

After what feels like minutes of us staring at each other with pure hatred, Theo steps around me to walk away, but the red haze has fogged my vision. The sting of rejection is fresh on my wounds and my egotistical self will not let her get away with this.

She's my goddamn prisoner after all.

As she steps around me, I raise my right hand, my large palm clenching around the back of her neck, dragging her back to the wall whilst my left hand grips her wet hair and pulls it tightly, exposing more of her neck to me. She gasps at the aggressive movement, her eyes blazing like an out of control fire.

She's mad, but I'm pissed.

"Remember your fucking place, sweetheart," I spit at her and after a beat, she has the audacity to smirk.

"And where's that, King? In the shower room with Puck? In your shower? On your face? Fucking tell me my place and maybe I'll stay there." The venom in her voice is powerful, but she just woke a bull from a nightmare and my rage is at an all-time high.

I pull her forwards by her throat before tugging back down on her hair, forcing her back to arch and her head to dip lower. The spray of the shower floods her face, drowning her features.

She blinks multiple times, trying to get the continuous spray of water droplets from her eyes, her mouth's dribbling with water as she coughs and tries to resist the pummelling spray making its way past her lips.

God, am I sick, or does she look sexy?

"Your place is with all the fucking lowlifes and scum in that prison. I took pity on you today. Don't mistake me for someone who will do it again."

Fighting for breath under the spray, I pull her head to the side to avoid her swallowing any water, and she takes a deep breath.

"I know you want me, King. Look at you." She looks down at my dick, which is throbbing for attention, digging into her stomach. "You gonna let one of them touch me, huh? You're gonna let one of them taste me, too?"

She's provoking me, but I'm the master of this game.

"Let them, baby. I've tasted pussy far sweeter than yours, sweetheart. You ain't nothing special."

I release her hair and throat with a firm shove, pushing her back into the wall, watching her slide down it and turning away from her. The flicker of hurt in her eyes is burning a hole through my chest, but I'm too riled up to care.

I'm lying, of course. Her pussy was the sweetest thing that's ever touched my tongue, a flavour I could cherish forever and never get tired of. My last meal on earth before I die could be the salty wetness of her cum and I'd die a happy man. But fuck if I let her know that.

I slam the door shut loudly behind me as I enter the study, wiping my hands down my face.

"Fuck!" I shout, a moment of shame unleashing from me.

"Am I interrupting something?" Dax says from the corner of the room, an eyebrow raised in amusement.

Realising I'm naked, I cover myself with my hand, not out of self-consciousness, but I'm sure Dax doesn't want to see my dick right now.

"No, we're leaving," I spit as I hastily grab a pair of trousers from a drawer.

"What about the girl?" Dax replies, nodding towards the bathroom.

"Fuck if I care. Get a guard to take her back to her bloody cell where she belongs."

Dax's eyebrow rises even higher, considering it's almost at his hairline already. I'm glad he's finding this amusing.

"Oh, fuck off," I spit, the rage inside me still boiling.

This girl is fucking me up.

# 14.
## Theo

I crawl up against the wall, hugging my legs to my chest, and bury my head into my knees, trying to fight the wave of emotion enveloping me. I take in big breaths, trying to calm myself down, my lungs burning from the pressure of trying to hold my breath under the spray of the shower.

What's the bastard trying to do? Fucking drown me?

I can't keep up with him. One minute he's hot, like boiling hot water that's scalding to the touch, but within seconds he freezes, colder than ice. I can't do right from wrong.

He leaves me in the shower after giving me some emotion. A passionate moment that I've never shared with anybody before. But to come barging back, basically demanding he take me like a rag doll after dismissing me so easily. I just can't keep up with him. What does he want from me?

He said he's had pussy far sweeter, so why does he put us both through this turmoil?

The shower starts to go cold when the door reopens and I lift my head, readying myself for another round of fighting, when my favourite face peeks around the door. Seeing Puck,

I lose it. My tears fall and as soon as he scoops me into his arms, I cling on like I'll never let go.

I refuse to give King any more of me. He doesn't get my tears, my body, my words, my soul. I'm done.

Puck covers my naked body with a towel and shuts off the shower, walking me away from the room. He doesn't ask what's happened. He's just there for me.

Like always.

ONCE WE GET BACK to the cells, after being ushered by another guard, who was fortunately holding a clean jumpsuit for me, Puck leads me down to an area of the prison I've not been to whilst my cell gets cleaned up from the blood and the dead human who's currently occupying it.

If you could call him human anyway.

It's a common room of sorts, some chairs lining up against the walls and tables dotted about here and there. There are a few inmates in here and some of them rake their eyes over my small form, but they know not to come near me with Puck by my side.

The room is cold and dimly lit, the same horrible glow of the light bulb lighting the space as best as it can. God, what wouldn't I do for some daylight.

Puck walks us over to the corner where five chairs sit, three of them occupied by men. The eldest of the men nods at Puck and subtly at me. He has shoulder-length hair that's either really greasy or wet from a shower. I can't tell. He's skinny, super skinny, and even slouched on his chair, I can tell he'd tower over me.

The man to his right stands and shakes Puck's hand with that tap to the back men do. He turns to me and smiles a toothless grin and I cringe, a little uncomfortable, unable to decide if his smile is genuine or seedy.

Then finally, the last man slouches on his chair, legs spread out in front of him, taking up a load of space, scowling at Puck.

"Theo, this is Sandy and Ty," Puck introduces the first two men, the lanky one being Sandy and the toothless guy Ty. "And this prick is Mac."

The other man sits up and leans over towards Puck, the scowl still in place.

"Fuck off, Puck."

Puck laughs and sits down on a chair, holding my hand and letting me decide if I'm comfortable. I love him for it, I really do.

"Would you believe he's mad because he lost an arm wrestle against me?" Puck snickers.

I raise my eyebrows and look over at Mac as a small chuckle leaves my lips.

"How incredibly cliché of you."

The other men laugh and Puck pulls me down next to him on the squeaky plastic chair.

"Don't knock our entertainment, beautiful, we are stuck in a prison after all," Sandy says, reaching his hand out to me. I look down at his outstretched hand and hesitate for a couple seconds before I shake it, letting Puck introduce me to his friends. Ty shakes my hand too and after a glare from Puck, Mac offers me his hand.

The men fall into easy conversation, throwing about names of people I don't know and I just sit there, silently observing each man as they converse. Mac soon cheers up after Puck promises him a rematch and I roll my eyes.

"How are you holding up, doll?" Ty asks me out of the blue and my eyes turn to his, deciding how to answer his question.

This morning I've gone from being assaulted, to having King's face on my pussy, to being abandoned in his shower. How am I holding up?

"Well, yanno," I start, looking at Sandy, "we are stuck in a prison, after all."

All the men laugh, and I relax my shoulders and take this moment for what it is. Life is never going to be the same, especially here, so what else can I do? Puck squeezes my hand and for the rest of the afternoon, we sit and chat with Sandy, Ty, and Mac and act like normal people.

It's like a little pocket of bliss, in a prison of all places, and my smile doesn't leave my face the entire time.

WALKING BACK into my cell with Puck, we enter to the strong stench of bleach. I look around and replay the scene in my head from hours ago, fiddling with my zip to make sure it's secured all the way at the top.

"I'm so sorry, T," Puck interrupts the silence and I look over at him, my eyebrows drawn together in confusion. "I should've been here. I wasn't here and I let you down."

"Puck, it wasn't your fault. Please don't blame yourself or apologise. I promise you I'm okay."

"But I should've been here. I'm always here!" He shakes his head and wipes a hand down his face, scanning his eyes around the small room.

"Puck." I hook my pinky finger in his. "I'm okay, I promise."

He nods and pulls me under his arm and, looking at our hooked pinkies, I'm reminded of King's bloody knuckles and Puck's bleeding nose.

"But whilst we're on the topic, where were you?" I turn, studying his nose. But Puck just chuckles.

"Let's just say you're not the only one King has a problem with sometimes." He winks.

Before I can say any more, there's a loud announcement, one I've not heard since arriving here, and I swear, my whole body comes alive.

"Courtyard!"

Puck smiles. "Are you ready to go outside?"

I'm practically bouncing off the walls at the opportunity to go outdoors. I miss the sunlight, the fresh air. I can't wait to breathe it into my lungs. Puck walks next to me, laughing the whole way as we travel through various corridors like the ones I arrived in.

"What do you think the weather is going to be like? I hope it's sunny and bright and hurts my eyes as soon as I step out there. Oh, but what if it's nighttime? Fuck, this is so exciting!" I squeak and Puck shakes his head at me.

"You're easily amused, T."

"Puck, are you kidding me right now? We get to go outside!"

In the next moment, a large metal security door opens ahead of us and we step out into a small courtyard. The sun is setting and the sky is downcast, rain splattering on the pavement.

I run. I don't think about anything but running into the cold wind and harsh raindrops. I lift my arms, like all the cliché rom coms, and turn my face up to the rain, staring at the grey clouds, a huge smile stretching my face.

Puck appears at my front and wipes the wet hair off my forehead.

"I'm sorry it's not sunny, Theo," Puck says, smiling at my happiness.

"That's okay, this is better."

We stand in the small square courtyard, prisoners surrounding us from all angles, bright spotlights illuminating the area, but after all the shit I've been through today, this week—hell, even my whole life—this moment right now is one of my favourites.

"Besides, it might be sunny next time." I smile and hook my pinkie finger through his. "Shall we bet on it?"

"You're on, T."

I laugh and look at Puck's smile, grateful to have him in here with me. Silver linings and all that.

## 15. King

The drive back to the Rhivers mansion was unbearable. Dax insisted on driving because according to him, my foul mood would get us killed. Anger is an emotion I know very well. Anger has consumed me since I was young.

Losing my mother after only having her for four years of my life is something no child should ever go through. To lose your sister, the most loving relative you have and a possible niece or nephew just over a decade later is pain beyond measure that no human being should have to endure. To find out that the reason for both their deaths was by the hand of the man who raised you.

The whole thing should be fictional. Something you read about or see in movies. But growing up in the world of the mafia and the shadow of the biggest and baddest... it was my reality.

Anger consumed me. My rage was focused and centred on avenging my mother and sister. But being a naive seventeen-year-old had no match for Carlo Rhivers. It was then that I learned where the District leaders' income came from.

The District Prison. Buried away for the criminals who they deemed fit for it, innocent or guilty, including me.

I push the thought out of my mind, not wanting to relive the year I endured in that very same hell hole I'm guilty of placing Theo in. Of where I'm guilty of keeping Puck.

Instead, my mind drifts back to Theo and my first memory of her, only weeks before I ended up in that very same cell of hers.

But the thought pains me, to hear her voice, innocent and oblivious to what was going on around her. Theo was the same age as my sister but had a much easier life. Consumed by my anger over the years, I had a rage built up for Theo.

A beautiful sixteen-year-old girl, the daughter of a District leader, yet she lived a happy, easy, guilt-free life. But my sister, who was in the exact same position, was shunned from existence, forced to hide her whole life to pay the ultimate price for falling in love and becoming pregnant.

Why was that fair?

But for a short, sweet moment, Theo had simmered the anger that brewed inside me and every day that followed—until Bonnie's death and the day I was locked up. Then by the time I got back, she was gone.

I shake my head of the past, trying to forget all the pent-up emotion surrounding my feelings towards Theo. She didn't deserve me or my life then and she definitely doesn't deserve it now.

Dax doesn't speak to me the whole drive home, letting me suffer in silence. The car slows down as we turn onto the estate of the Rhivers mansion.

The long driveway stretches out way ahead of us behind the huge iron gates, the gravel softly crunching underneath the tyres as we draw closer to my home.

Dax turns the steering wheel, manoeuvring the car around the large fountain before coming to a stop at the bottom of the marble stairs leading to the front door. I stare out the tinted window up at the large double doors, the famous R staking its claim as the mansion of the Rhivers family.

"Time to rule the empire, cuz," Dax says, his voice rough from not speaking for over an hour.

I nod and clear my head, unbuckling my seat belt.

I'm now the leader of the First District, whether people like it or not, and I'm going to do a better job than my father ever did.

I jump out of the car and stalk up the stairs, Dax a beat behind me. The huge guard hovering in front of the door nods and hastily opens the door for my entrance.

Ignoring him, I push my way through and head straight for my room. I need to clean up.

"Sir," a timid, quiet voice calls out as I'm halfway up the stairs. I pause mid-step and turn to the 'assistant' my father always used, in more ways than one. I didn't even know her name. I just look at her, urging her to continue.

"Welcome home, sir. Kennedy Harlow and Edison Ramon are waiting to see you."

I roll my eyes. I knew I wouldn't be able to postpone it any longer, but I was hoping for at least one night home before dealing with the other District leaders, especially Theo's father.

"I'm going to freshen up. They can wait in my study."

The assistant nods and scurries off, and I make a mental note to dismiss her as soon as I can—she won't be of any use to me.

I undress immediately and climb into the shower, ridding away the past twenty-four hours.

My mind drifts back to my shower with Theo, devouring her sweet pussy, trying to fuck her and being rejected. I groan in defeat and smack my fist against the tiled wall. Sixteen-year-old Theo hovers in my mind, behind my eyelids, smiling up at me like I was the only person in the world to ever make her smile. I punch the tiles again. I haven't thought about that time of my life in many years, but everything with Theo now has it simmering right on the surface, ready to spill out.

*Enough now.*

I climb out of the shower and put on a fresh suit, ready for my meeting with the District leaders.

---

DAX IS WAITING for me outside of the study doors and he pats me on the back as I approach him. We both give each other the same look. A look that if you weren't us, you wouldn't know what it meant. But we did.

*Let's fucking do this.*

We both open a door each and stride in together and with one hand, I do up the buttons on my blazer and overlook my guests without meeting either of their eyes. I head straight for the seat at the head of my desk, Dax still in step with me.

The thing about me and Dax is we're in this together. I may be the official leader of the First District, but Dax is still my equal, and everyone better learn that sooner rather than later.

Rather than sitting, I choose to stand, looking down at Kennedy Harlow and Edison Ramon, who I see has also brought his second with him. Edison's cousin, Casper, is a very secretive, quiet man who seems to follow Edison around like a second shadow.

Like me and Dax.

I've never thought anything of it before, but the man seems useless. Never says a word, just stands still. At least Dax has my back.

"Gentlemen." I nod at all three of them, getting nods in return.

"How's my daughter holding up, King?" Kennedy Harlow says, surprising me with his interest.

"I couldn't give a fuck how she's holding up, Kennedy," I say with a bored expression. We're not here to talk about Theodora Harlow.

"Fair enough." He shrugs with a small smile. The grin is evil and full of hate, and I wonder how his relationship with Theo must have been. I know he never let her off the grounds, but they got on as far as I knew. But then again, he was quick to pass her over into my clutches.

"Son, in this situation, not that we thought it would ever come to this, we would go through business with you. Give you the intel on the prison and so on. But since you already know about it, there's no need," Kennedy speaks, as if he's in charge here. My anger is back and it's directed all at him.

"Firstly, I'm not your son. Be sure not to call me that again."

Kennedy raises his eyebrows at my outburst. *Good.*

"Secondly, I worked closely with my father for many years. True, I may not know a lot of the ins and outs, but for now, I know all that I need to know. And with all due respect, Mr Harlow, I don't need you to come in here and try to tell me how to do my job. Me and Dax here have everything under control. I am not my father and I will do a damn better job at this than he ever did. This is my throne now. Don't forget that."

Kennedy narrows his eyes slightly before slouching in his seat, shrugging his shoulders.

"So I can see."

I pour each man a shot of whiskey and offer the glasses to them before pouring myself and Dax one.

"Mr Rhivers, our relationship between the First and Second Districts has been very platonic and we wish to keep it that way," Edison speaks after swallowing his mouthful.

"Of course, Edison. I have no bad blood between any of you and have no desire to jeopardise that."

Edison nods in response, but Kennedy continues to stare at me, swirling the liquid around in his glass.

Dax cuts the tension between us, talking more about business.

"We will continue to monitor and run the prison with the exact same secrecy as always. It has been a successful income for many years now, but business has been slow. We've only recently added a new inmate, so we need to think up some strategies on how to increase this. On the topic of our newest inmate, Mr Harlow, you owe your half for her placement."

I turn my head to Dax with speed, Kennedy not far behind, darting his gaze to Dax.

"Excuse me?" Kennedy replies, looking as stunned as I feel.

"Mr Harlow—"

"It's Kennedy," he interrupts.

"Kennedy," Dax continues. "You wanted Miss Theodora Harlow in the District Prison. As a member of your family and strictly your preference for wanting her in there, you need to pay, just like everyone else." Dax has some balls, but nevertheless, he's right.

"I believe what I said was 'she was all yours,'" Kennedy retorts.

"And what exactly did you mean by that, Mr Harlow? Because we are under the impression you wanted her there."

Kennedy growls at Dax, probably for calling him Mr Harlow after being asked to call him by his first name.

"She's all yours meant she's all yours, kid. Do with that what you will, but I'm not spending any of my pocket on her when she was supposed to be making me money in the first place." Kennedy is raging and as much as I'm enjoying him coming undone, I can't get past what he's just said.

"What do you mean she was supposed to be making you money?" My question confuses him as he must've realised he's slipped up on something.

"None of your business, boy. Look, I'm not paying anything for that stupid girl to be anywhere," he retaliates.

My fists clench by my sides. What was he going to make her do for money? And why do I care?

Very calmly, Dax jumps back in before I can do something stupid.

"Very well. We shall bring her back here where she can

remain part of the Rhivers family. She would be great company for Aurora."

I look at Dax, astounded. Bring her to live here! *Is he out of his fucking mind?*

"You seem to have a habit of finding lost girls and giving them some sort of life, Dax. Tell me, what is it about them? Their vulnerability, their lack of respect, their pussy?"

Dax's fists clench by his sides and I have to put a stop to this now. Insulting Theo, his own daughter, is bad enough. But one thing Dax won't stand for is disrespect for his girl.

"Mr Harlow, this meeting is over. You have until the end of the month to pay for your share of Theodora. Let's not start a feud now after so many years, hmm?" I cut in, ending the discussion.

Kennedy is fuming, his shoulders rising rapidly as he considers his next move. Lucky for him, he picks the right one and nods, then turns to leave the study. I watch the dust float through the air in his wake.

"Mr Rhivers," Edison says to both myself and Dax, shaking our hands. "This meeting aside, we're happy to be working with you and look forward to continuing our partnership. As always, if you need anything, let me know what I can do."

I thank him and shake Casper's hand also as they leave. At least we can rely on them if things go south with Kennedy and the Second District.

Me and Dax stand in silence. My mind is moving a mile a minute, trying to make sense of everything that happened.

Before I can utter a word to Dax, the large wooden door opens and I roll my eyes at the interruption.

Can we not catch a break?

But once I see who's standing at the door, my guard drops, relaxing instantly, Dax's posture following mine in suit.

"Will you ever learn to mind your own business, Aurora?" I say, smiling at the innocent eyes in front of me.

Her wicked smile grows from ear to ear and she winks. "Never."

"Rori!" Dax breathes, finally feasting his eyes on his girl after so many days and an inkling of guilt festers inside that I kept him away for so long.

"Hey, baby, miss me?" She cheers, running into Dax's open arms, her silvery hair, long and half-plaited, blowing behind her in her wake.

Knowing when I'm not needed, I leave them to it, happy Dax has finally got his little birdie back in his arms.

But I still can't take my mind off of what Dax said.

Bring Theo here? No chance!

# 16.
# Theo

It's been roughly four months since I was put in the District Prison.

*Four months.*

I've lost a sufficient amount of weight from the lack of food and my complexion is disgruntled and pale. The bags under my eyes swallow my skin like dark shadows.

After that first week of being here and they let us out into the small courtyard on that cold, rainy day, it's my favourite time of the week, seeing the sky, whether cloudy or clear. It is my saving grace, something to look forward to.

Predicting the weather is one of my favourite things to think about. One of the *only* things to think about. The satisfaction of being right, the pleasant surprise of being wrong. I don't care. I embraced the outdoors for every three thousand and six hundredth seconds I had it each week. An hour wasn't long enough and Puck ended up having to drag me back inside every time.

Puck is still my protector. My friend. With nothing to do but talk, me and Puck spend every second we're awake doing just that. We speak about my home, my mother, his Bonnie, and what it was like growing up in the Rhivers mansion. He even joined in on my weather game sometimes.

After being introduced to Sandy, Ty, and Mac, they often joined us. Puck would laugh and joke with them, and I would sit in silence, wishing sometimes they would leave us alone. But I had nothing to worry about. Puck promised me I was his best friend with our pinky swear, my child-like brain being easy to please these days considering I have no other expectations.

Sandy, Mac, and Ty soon became my friends of sorts—but only when I was with Puck. I wouldn't dare go near them without him. Since that third day here when I was manhandled by that creep, Puck is with me at all times.

Since he helped pick me up from King's bathroom with another guard, up to this very second, he's only left my side to sleep.

Much to my dismay. I'd rather have him with me for that, too.

Another thing I can never seem to take my mind off is King. I haven't seen him since our bathroom escapade and my hatred and anger for him seem to grow more and more each day. How can he go from being sweet and caring, tracing my scars with gentle fingers, licking me up with pure lust, to advancing on me like a predator about to destroy his prey, all traces of respect and kindness gone?

Just the devil ready to take away another soul he'd used to make vulnerable.

And then he leaves. He doesn't come back.

Was I just going to be an easy fuck for him?

I've seen Dax a few times, coming and going, checking

on the 'prison' as he says. I know he's checking on me but why? King clearly doesn't give a fuck.

I've thought about our past more than I'd like to admit, and how I came to know King Rhivers, and it's been eating away at me. I don't want to tell Puck and let it out in the open. It feels so secretive. It *was* secretive. And now it's nothing. *We're nothing.*

But there was something about King that day that reminded me so much of the boy I once knew.

While lying with Puck, the comfort of his arms around me, I allow myself to think about it once more, as it's too exhausting trying not to.

*The heat in the car is stuffy and suffocating, the tiny crack in the window doing nothing to aid the air circulation. I know Dad said to wait in the car, but I can't stand it anymore. I open the door and step out into the sunlight, letting the fresh air consume my lungs. I take a deep breath in and wipe my sweaty forehead with the back of my hand.*

*I look around, taking in all of my surroundings, and I recognise the huge building in front of me from photos. This is the Rhivers mansion.*

*So we are in the First District.*

*I spin around and see a large fountain behind the parked car, with water spouting out from all sides in perfect unison. I head over to it and dip my hand into the water, then bring my wet hand to my face, cooling myself down. Turning back to the house, I sit on the edge of the fountain and admire the towering building and the beautiful gardens that surround it.*

There's a huge guard standing at the doorway, and a few scattered around the long driveway, but aside from the gentle breeze and the water spraying, there is no other movement. It's peaceful.

My father said he had last-minute business to attend to on our way back from a visit he's dragged me to that he said was also for 'business'.

I'm never allowed to go on business trips with him or to interrupt him whilst he works at home. But today is different.

He introduced me to Edison Ramon, the leader of the Third District, and lots of other men that I didn't know, and I had to shake all their hands. They gave me funny smiles that made me uncomfortable. My father told me it was fine. I wish my mother could have come with us, but she was too tired. Or so my father said.

On the way home from the Third District, he took a detour and we ended up at the Rhivers mansion. All I really want is to go home.

"Hi." A male voice makes me jump and I lose my balance, one hand falling in the fountain to stop my whole body from following it.

The person responsible, a young boy around my age, curses, then jumps forward to steady my balance, pulling me up and away from the water.

"Thank you," I whisper, averting my eyes to look down at the ground.

"Uhh, you okay?" he questions, dipping his head, trying to get a better look at me.

"Yeah, I'm fine," I reply, trying to be brave, but a small quiver in my voice gives me away.

*Truth is, I've never really spoken to anyone my own age, apart from Emerson, who is still a few years older than me.*

"I'm King," he says, standing tall.

*My eyes lock on him as I connect the dots. King? Carlo Rhivers' son? His eyes are a deep forest green and his smile is just as unruly as his wavy hair, a dark brown mess atop his head.*

"King," I repeat like an echo, suddenly feeling a lot like Tarzan meeting Jane for the first time. *Internally, I'm face-planting to the ground.*

"Yes, that's my name."

"I know who you are," I say quickly, trying to redeem myself.

*He smirks and raises one eyebrow.*

"Is that so?" He winks. *My cheeks heat and I can feel the rosy tint exposing my embarrassment.*

"Everyone knows who you are." I shrug, acting nonchalant. *He chuckles and it makes my heart beat faster. He seems taken aback by his sudden outburst and coughs to regain himself.*

"And who am I talking to?" he asks, cocking his head to one side.

"Theo." *I smile, not wanting to tell him my last name. He's King Rhivers, while I am not important in the slightest.*

"Theo," he mimics, like I did to him earlier.

*King places his hand on his chest.*

"King." *He then extends his arm and places his hand gently on my shoulder.* "Theo." *He winks again.*

*I laugh out loud at his Tarzan impression, slightly embarrassed he thought the same thing as me, but strangely relaxed and comfortable around him. King sits on the edge of the* fountain where I was only moments ago and sighs. Feeling brave, I sit down next to him, my arm ever so slightly close to his.

"What's wrong?" I ask. I don't expect him to tell me anything, but there's no harm in asking.

"What isn't?" he says back with a shrug. I turn my head and study his face, starting with those dark green eyes and ending on his soft pink lips. I'm not sure how long I was staring before King breaks the silence.

"Like what you see, Theo?" he teases, his tongue peeking out slightly to lick his bottom lip. My breath catches and I'm caught off guard, not knowing how to respond.

My cheeks heat up again—I'll be as red as a tomato before I leave.

He laughs again, this time letting it relax his features, and he nudges my arm with his.

"Relax, Theo. You don't have to say anything. Your blush is giving it all away." With that, my cheeks go redder and King bursts out into laughter. Real laughter. I like seeing him like this, but it was my ego that was paying the price for it.

Without a second thought, I playfully push him, with every intention of him ending up in the water behind us. King, completely caught off guard, falls backwards with a huge splash in the shallow water. This time, I laugh uncontrollably as he sits there, soaked to the bone. At first, I can't decide if he's mad. The ghost of his smile remains while he considers what to do.

"I suppose I deserved that." He chuckles and makes his way to standing.

"I'd offer to help you out, but I know how that goes," I say through my laughter, not stupid enough to fall for that one.

"It's all right, you don't have to."

Instead, he wraps his arm around my shoulders and pulls my back flush against his chest, dragging me backwards until I land with a splash in front of him.

I laugh. I laugh so much my cheeks hurt.

I haven't felt like this in such a long time. King is laughing too, his arm still firmly around my chest.

As I calm down, I'm suddenly very aware of his hand inches away from my breast and my breathing picks up. I'm sure he can feel my heart rate spike as he quickly removes his arm.

I turn around and look up at King, who is smiling down at me. He brushes some of my wet hair away from my forehead, setting it right, the gesture way too romantic for real life, especially my life. This kind of thing only happens in the books I read.

King leans in closer and whispers in my ear, "Why are you here, Theo? Where have you been?"

I look into his eyes, my stomach fluttering with a million butterflies I can't control.

"I..."

"Theodora Harlow!" my father's voice booms through the peaceful air, and I flinch away from King. He looks up at my father approaching us, running down the marble steps of the mansion. "What do you think you're doing, kid? Get in the goddamn car!"

He's angry. My father has never shouted at me like that before.

"You're Theo Harlow? Kennedy Harlow's daughter?" King says quietly as we both stand.

I nod timidly and try to gracefully climb out of the fountain, my white sundress now completely soaked through. I look down at myself, my basic nude bra showing itself through my now transparent dress. King looks too and I blush again, but this time not from embarrassment.

"Theo!" my father shouts again, and I jump on the spot.

I turn to run for the door when King grabs my hand.

"I'll see you again, Theo." He gives me his famous wink once again, water droplets glistening on his skin, and I smile. If moments like these are what I've been missing out on, I don't ever want to go home again.

"I hope so," I whisper before running to the car and climbing in, trying to ignore my father's grunts from the front seat about me soaking the leather. I turn around and look out the back window. King stands there, hands in his pockets, dripping wet, and I smile.

I WAKE UP SOMETIME AFTER, realising I fell asleep in Puck's arms, and I sigh at the memory that consumed me before looking up into Puck's blue eyes. He's already awake and looking down at me.

"Hey." I snuggle my head closer to his chest, nesting in the crook of his neck.

"T?" he says.

"Mhmm?" I mumble, ready to fall into another nap already.

"There's someone here to see you." He sounds cautious and I roll my eyes.

"Dax, you checked on me yesterday. What now?" I groan, turning in Puck's arms and stiffening instantly when I see King sitting on Puck's stool right in front of us.

"Theodora."

I grip on to Puck, the memory from when we were teens resurfacing, same as the one from months ago when he up and left after savagely trying to take me. Puck must sense my unease as he brings his hand to mine, hooking his pinkie finger with mine. *He's got me.*

"Piss off," I spit at King, turning my back on him and staring holes into Puck's chest.

"Unfortunately, sweetheart, you're coming with me."

I turn my head back around and throw daggers at him.

"I'm going fucking nowhere with you!" My defiance riles him up. Good, he's made me feel like this for months.

Months of waiting for him to come back, to apologise, to just fucking say hello, anything. Months of anger brewing just below the surface of being disrespected and abandoned. I'm not going anywhere with him.

King stands up and throws the stool to the corner of the cell, making me flinch, and stalks towards us. In one swift movement, he bends down and hooks his arms under my legs and back, lifting me over his shoulder in a fireman's hold and wrenching me away from Puck. I kick and scream at him, but it makes no difference. King's holding me so tight, there's no way I can break free.

"Puck! PUCK!" I scream out for him, hoping he won't let King take me.

"T, I've got you!" he replies and holds his pinkie finger up, and I can't help it, but the tears flow.

In all the months since King left me in his bathroom, I haven't let myself cry once. But the dam has burst and the tidal wave has broken through.

I kick and cry and punch and cry, Puck getting blurrier and further away with every second.

"I've got you, T!" Puck shouts one last time before I can no longer see him. And I give up kicking and punching and screaming. I just drop my head and let the silent tears take over, soaking the back of King's suit.

## 17. King

Theo slouches in the chair, her gorgeous figure now small and fragile. It could be the dim lighting of the interrogation room, but her skin is pale and gloomy, her eyes have lost their sparkle, and her cheeks are stained with fresh tears that continue to fall silently.

Fuck, carrying her away from Puck like that was torture. I knew she'd be pissed to see me, but I didn't expect that. Her punches came hard and fast to my back, her screams so loud in my ear, I was ready to drop her and never touch her again.

"Theo." I break the silence, clearing my throat. I stayed away this long because she was a weakness and a distraction I didn't need. I won't let it go back to that.

Theo continues to look at the floor, her shoulders hunched forward, her arms limp, and I can see the tears dropping onto the floor by her feet.

I soften my tone and crouch in front of her, gently lifting her chin up with my fingers.

Her eyes lock on mine, and a powerful emotion washes over me as I stare back into her watery eyes, full of sadness.

"Theo," I almost whisper, flattening my hand on her cheek.

She flinches away from my touch and within seconds, she spits at me, pure disgust coating her almost unrecognisable face. I recoil from her retaliation and wipe her spit off my cheek with my sleeve.

She doesn't back down, her eyes burning a hole straight through me. I stand and look at her from above, reminding her who's in charge here.

Theo starts to stand, but my hand pushes down on her shoulder, forcing her back into the chair.

"DON'T FUCKING TOUCH ME!" Theo screams, slapping my hand away and falling to the floor. She buries her head in her hands and sobs again.

I'm way out of my depth here. I have no idea how to handle her. How am I supposed to get any information out of her if she reacts like this every time I talk to her or touch her?

Fuck this. I'm in charge here and I'm done pussyfooting around her because of her mood swings.

"Sit in the fucking chair, Theodora, or so help me God, I will sit you in it myself," I warn, hoping the threat of touching her will be enough to get her to listen to me.

She scoffs, but as I take a step closer, she scurries to her feet and sits back in the chair, bringing her knees up and hugging them to her chest as her feet dangle off the edge of the chair.

"Do you get off on this?" she spits at me.

"Excuse me?" I question.

"This sick game you play. You hate me, you want me, you want to fuck me, you fucking hate me again. You leave, you come back. What the fuck is with you? How long till you're back next time, huh?"

Theo drops her legs and is on the verge of standing again, so I take another step closer.

"If your ass leaves that seat again, Theo, I will cuff you to it."

There's a challenge in her eyes, but I know she won't act on it, not after the way she reacted to my touch before.

"Do you get off on that too, huh?"

I lean down so my face is only inches from hers.

"If I *got off* on you, Theodora, don't you think I would've come back for you over the past four months?" I sneer, letting my disgust for her show on my face.

I stand and turn away from her, trying to hide the truth in my eyes. That is the exact reason why I couldn't come back. Because I *did* want her.

"Fuck you!" she shouts, standing up, the chair scraping across the floor as she lunges at me.

Has she learnt nothing?

In one smooth motion, I take out the handcuffs from behind my suit jacket and grip Theo's wrist as she raises it to hit me, attaching the cuff to her wrist.

"Get off me!" she screams over and over, trying to slither out of my hold.

I drag her back over to the chair and attach the spare handcuff to the back of it.

"I fucking hate you!"

"And I fucking told you not to get off that goddamn chair!" I shout back.

Theo flinches, the anger and volume echoing around the small room. She's breathing hard and fast, her chest rising and falling heavily, getting slower with each second.

"Uncuff me," she says calmly.

"No," I simply reply.

"You can't treat me like this," she retorts.

"In case you're missing something, sweetheart, I can treat you however I damn well please. You're in my prison. You're in my possession. You're *my* fucking prisoner. There's no one else here to save you. You. Are. Mine!"

Her jaw drops at my revelation and I realise how it sounded, but whatever way she takes it, it's the truth. Whether I want her or not, she's in my prison, so she's mine.

"I don't belong to anyone, King," she murmurs.

"The money in my pocket from your father buying your place here states otherwise."

Her head jerks up fast, her eyes narrowing at me. The truth is, Kennedy Harlow still hasn't paid his full amount for Theo's keep and the bastard will be dead soon if he doesn't cash in. I'm not running an orphanage where he can just drop off his unwanted child. He will pay me what he owes or he will pay with his life.

"Now, whilst we're on the topic of your father, I need you to tell me what you were doing for him to get him a hefty sum of money," I tell her, crossing my arms over my chest. "And you better think twice before lying to me."

"What the fuck are you talking about?" Theo asks, looking perplexed.

After Kennedy announced Theo was supposed to be making him money, I've looked into Kennedy Harlow as much as I could. He gets a hefty cheque every week from an anonymous sender that I still haven't found. We're talking thousands, but all I've been able to figure out is that it arrives in his bank every Friday evening at 11:00 p.m. There's never been a subject until last night when attached to the payment was a message from the sender.

'No more until you can promise her.'

This has to have something to do with Theo, whether she knows anything or not, so I jumped straight into my car and hauled ass to the prison to interrogate her.

"Theodora, I won't ask you again."

"I haven't been doing shit for my father. I've been stuck in here for fuck's sake."

"Don't play smart with me."

She huffs, rolling her eyes. "I'm not playing smart, King. I've been in here for four months and before that I was trapped in my fucking room at home half the time. What do you honestly think I could be doing with my father for money?"

She makes a lot of sense, but I need to be a hundred percent sure.

"Maybe becoming a hitman and murdering Carlo Rhivers?" I accuse.

"You're shitting me, right? You think of all the people in the Districts, my father, Kennedy Harlow, hired *me*, his pathetic daughter who wasn't allowed to leave the grounds, to kill Rhivers?" she questions. When she puts it like that, it does sound ridiculous.

"Then why did you kill him, if it wasn't for your father or for money?"

It's a long shot. Dax still hasn't been able to find out why she killed my father.

She sighs and doesn't utter another word for almost a full minute. The silence is deafening.

"I didn't kill Carlo for money or for my father," she starts, hesitating before continuing. "I... I did it for revenge, for justice."

"Why?" I question. It makes no sense. What would Carlo have done to her to give her ammo for his murder?

"Because he killed my mother," she says, looking straight into my eyes. The revelation surprises me, but I don't let it show.

"How? Your mother drowned, Theodora. She killed herself."

Theo sits on the floor, shaking her head, her arm propped up higher than the rest of her body whilst it's cuffed to the back of the chair.

"She didn't kill herself. Carlo killed her." Her voice is harsh and certain. There's no doubt in my mind that Theo believes what she's saying.

"Prove it." I can't deny it's something he would've done had he had motive, but why?

"There isn't any proof. I just know," Theo whispers. She must realise how ridiculous she sounds without the proof, but that's not the matter at hand right now. I need to know what Kennedy Harlow is playing at.

"Regardless, Theodora, I need to know why your father is making a lot of money where you're concerned," I reply firmly.

"King, I swear I don't know. I've barely had anything to do with my father the past two years. Since we lost Mum, I don't even know the man anymore, if I ever did."

I don't want to tell her the conclusion Dax and I have drawn.

What if I tell her and it's all been part of some grander

plan? I'd be playing right into their hands. But what if it's not?

The look in her eyes, the defeat in her voice, tell me all I need to know. I believe her. And that's the reason I choose to come clean.

"Then I have reason to believe he was going to sell you."

## 18.
## Theo

"Excuse me?" I try to stand, but the chair drags heavily behind me, my hand still cuffed to the back of it. I still can't believe that bastard cuffed me to the chair.

"I believe your father was going to sell you," King replies calmly, as if he hasn't just dropped a massive bomb on me.

"And why do you have reason to believe such a ridiculous assumption?"

"Your father admitted to me four months ago that you were supposed to be making money for him. He was refusing to pay for your keep here at the prison and disclosed that you should've been making money for him, not him having to be out of pocket because of you. I believed it was because he'd used you to kill Carlo. Whilst I think your claim of him murdering Elisa is absurd, I do believe that you didn't do it on your father's orders.

"I've been checking your father's accounts discreetly for months now and he gets a payment every Friday evening, for thousands, from an anonymous payer that I am yet to find out. Yesterday, they left a message to your father saying he wasn't getting any more payments until he can promise 'her'.

I believe the 'her' they're referring to is you and that you were going to be sold or something of that extent."

My mind moves at a hundred miles per hour, trying to process everything he's said.

"Theodora, this is all speculation, but I have enough to go on to believe it's what your father's planning. I just need to figure out who the anonymous payer is and what your father intends to do about it considering you're locked up in here. I'm going to see to it that I can guarantee your safety."

I laugh loudly, although none of this is funny in the slightest.

"Guarantee my safety? I'm in a fucking prison filled with men who try to attack me daily and in case you forgot, one nearly did. You can't guarantee my safety! Besides, why the fuck do you care?"

"I don't care, but I need to know what Kennedy is doing behind my back and you, alive, and in my possession, are my leverage."

Oh, charming. He needs me as a power play against my father. A pawn in a game I've never been allowed access to.

"As for your safety, you will be staying at the Rhivers mansion for the time being," he states calmly, as if he hasn't just announced something he knows will piss me off.

"Fuck no," I spit. He's got to be joking. There's no way I'm going to live in his place. No way!

"Theodora, your father knows many of the men within these walls and whilst no breach with him has ever happened before, I cannot take the risk that he won't get a hold of you in here. At my home, I can keep you under surveillance at all times. Safe and sound."

"No." I know this prison is a shit hole, but I have Puck as my safety net.

"If Kennedy is planning a business deal behind my back that encourages the selling of women, even if it is you or whoever else, then I won't let it slide. I run and oversee the Three Districts and I won't stand for it. I need you alive and safe for now whether I like it or not and that's final."

King turns his back on me and leaves me on the floor, still fucking handcuffed to this stupid chair. I try to gather my thoughts to make sense of everything that's been revealed in the past ten minutes.

My father was going to sell me to someone. King wants me to live at his house in case the prison gets infiltrated. Not because he cares, but because he wants me safe in his possession as leverage. I admitted to why I killed Carlo and he didn't even care. And now I have to go and live in his house.

Away from Puck.

I know I should be relieved, minus the recent revelations about my dad, but I'm scared. This prison is all I know now. Being with Puck is all I know now. I've never had a friend like him and I don't think I can go a day without him.

King played a back-and-forth game with me, then dropped me for months, and now he wants me to live with him, but as his goddamn prisoner still.

The door opens but instead of King, Dax strolls in. His eyes rake over my position, my head resting on my elevated arm.

"For fuck's sake," he mutters seeing my hand attached to the chair. "He couldn't even uncuff you before he left, huh?" He scoffs, his words more of a statement than a question.

Dax pulls out a set of keys before unlocking my hand

from the cuff.

"Thank you," I whisper as Dax sits down next to me on the dirty floor, not caring about dirtying up his expensive suit.

"Is it all true?" I ask, knowing Dax will speak to me like an actual human.

"It's what we assume," he says tactfully.

"I don't want to live there," I say, knowing it won't make any difference.

Dax looks at me, confusion knitting his brows together.

"You'd rather stay here?"

"Yes," I reply but feel like I need to explain my case. "Dax, I can't live there. I can't be near him like that. I hate him."

Dax laughs softly but lets me continue.

"I can't leave Puck. I won't. He's literally all I have now. I can't be a prisoner in his home. I did that in my own home for years. At least here, there's still an extent of freedom away from him. If I go with you, I'm just his property," I whisper, my defences dropping. I hate how weak I've become.

Dax nods, then after sitting in silence with me for a minute, he stands and leaves the room. I don't know what I'm supposed to do, so I just sit and wait. It feels like hours waiting by myself, but it must only be minutes before Puck walks through the door, his gaze sweeping over mine before holding his arms out and letting me run into them. Puck holds me tightly, letting my tears soak through his jumpsuit.

This is becoming a regular occurrence—I need to get a hold of myself.

"They're taking me away," I cry quietly into his chest

and Puck leans backwards slightly so he can look at me. "He wants me to live at the Rhivers mansion. He says he needs to guarantee my safety because my father is after me."

His brows furrow in confusion and I make a mental note to explain it properly if I ever get the chance.

"T, that's a good thing. You're getting out of here," he says reassuringly, rubbing his large hands up and down my arms to comfort me.

"Puck, I can't leave without you."

He laughs, the deep rumbles vibrating right through me as he holds me. "You're actually getting out of this fucking prison and you're worrying about me?"

"It's not like that, Puck, but I don't think I can actually live without you."

He chuckles again.

"That's very dramatic, even for you. Come on," he says and starts to back out the door of the small dark room, holding my hand securely. King and Dax are nowhere to be seen, so we make our way back to my cell. I know how ridiculous I sound, but this cell and Puck really are all I have now and I don't want to be without them, out in the unknown. I've been back and forth with King so many times. My father has dismissed and shunned me for years. I know I'm in captivity, with the never-ending danger that a predator will finally succeed in catching its prey. But even dying here is surely better than going back out there, forced to be lonely and isolated again. Right?

Puck opens my cell door and lets me inside before closing it and joining me on my shitty mattress, in the exact same position we were in before King took me away.

This is all I need.

# 19.
## Theo

I jolt awake and look around, taking in my surroundings, and instantly find relief when my eyes scan the familiar small room and Puck in his usual spot next to the gate. It's been three weeks since King came in and told me I was going to live in the Rhivers mansion, but luckily for me, in the most peculiar way, I'm still here.

I haven't seen or heard from King or Dax since they left me on my own in that small dark room where Puck came to get me. I don't understand why I'm still here as King made it very clear I wasn't staying.

Part of me wonders if Dax spoke to him after talking to me, but I still don't understand why King would go back on his word. Either way, I'm grateful. But every morning for the past three weeks, I've woken up frightened that I'm no longer here and I've been taken away against my will.

I have nightmares of faceless men taking me in the dead of night away from Puck. I wake up screaming and sweating but always hear Puck soothing me through the wall. He'll tell me stories. He'll count until I fall back asleep. He'll predict the weather for our next outing into the small yard—my favourite game.

But every night they come. And every morning I panic, until I know I'm still here.

Puck sighs and makes his way over to me, taking his place next to me as his arm curls around my shoulders.

His manly scent fills my nostrils and like always, I find comfort with him.

"Still not getting any better then?" he questions. "What are we going to do with you, hmm?" He soothes, rubbing softly at my arm.

"I don't know how to make it stop. I feel like I'm going crazy," I admit.

"You've gone through some crazy shit, T. Being in here for months, finding out what your father had planned, watching your back constantly in here. I'm surprised you haven't gone full batshit crazy yet." He chuckles.

"It's not funny," I mumble tiredly.

"I know." He smiles, kissing my forehead.

I told Puck everything King had told me back in that interrogation room when Puck brought me back to my cell. He didn't seem surprised.

*"I've seen the shit these men are capable of, T. Nothing surprises me anymore,"* he'd said.

I often think about a young Puck, only eighteen years old, living with the grief of losing his love and his unborn baby, only to be thrown in here to live out the rest of his days.

No one deserves that, especially not Puck. He has so much love to give. So much love already given to Bonnie and their baby and the rest now wasted because they're gone. It makes me so angry that Carlo Rhivers took that away from him.

Murdered his own daughter and grandchild because she fell pregnant.

Puck deserves the world and he deserves a life and love as great as he had. I won't rest until he gets it.

"Puck, if you could get out of here, what would you do?" I whisper.

He's quiet for many minutes, both of us thinking over my question.

"Honestly, T, I wouldn't have a clue."

I shuffle in his arms so I can look up at him.

"I've been in this shithole for so long, Theo, I don't even know what's out there anymore. But I know she isn't. I'm not sure if I could live my life fully, out in that world without her," he says with pain in his voice.

"But you could make a new life for yourself. Puck, you're only twenty-seven. You literally have a whole life ahead of you," I whimper softly, hurting for him.

"I know that. But I just can't see that life for me. Not since I've been here. It's never been an option. But being in here right now with you is the best kind of life I can ask for," Puck admits.

I hate that this is his life.

"You know, you remind me of her. I reckon she had a little something to do with you being here. Somehow she knew I'd need you in here to keep me sane."

I chuckle lightly, a lone tear slipping down my cheek.

"I think she would've sent you someone a little better than me. I'm here because I murdered Carlo Rhivers."

"Exactly." He winks at me, wiping the tears from my cheek.

I didn't just avenge my mother, but I avenged Bonnie

and their baby too, and I am goddamn fucking proud to have done it for them.

MORE DAYS FLY by with Puck's and my same routine, the nightmares and panic still haunting me every time I fall asleep. My body is weak and tired, and I'm starting to lose count of how long it's been.

We've just got back from the yard, soaking in the sunlight, and I feel a little more alive after the fresh air. We're sitting in my cell, me, Puck, Sandy, Mac, and Ty. I'm listening and laughing as they all share stories about each other from the years they've been here.

Yes, this is supposedly a prison for criminals, but after getting to know these guys, I've learnt that not everyone here is actually guilty of a crime. Puck being the biggest proof. Some of these men are just people in the wrong place at the wrong time. They don't deserve to be living out their life here. Except maybe Sandy—he's definitely suspicious.

Whilst Ty is halfway through a story about Mac getting locked in the shower room overnight, two big shadows appear at my cell gate, staring down at all five of us.

King and Dax stand tall in the open doorway, giving off no emotion. My memory shifts through every nightmare and minor panic attack I've had since I last saw them both and a funny feeling takes over, my palms clamming up at their sudden appearance.

"Say your goodbyes, Theodora. It's time to go," King says matter-of-factly as if he hadn't dropped a bomb on me.

"No!" I spit out, getting to my feet, the other men following suit. "You can't just come back here and demand I leave!"

"Yes, I can. I gave you some extra time and now it's really not safe. We need to leave," King replies before turning his back on me and Dax nods, following.

"What has changed in three fucking weeks, King?" I shout after him.

But the next few minutes happen in such a quick blur that I can't catch my breath.

King turns around, heading for me, his fists clenched, the anger busting through him as Dax tries to hold him back to calm him down before he comes for me all guns blazing.

Puck shouts my name in an agonisingly loud volume as he heads directly for me. Looking in his direction, I turn to see a large man running straight for me from behind, a huge knife held out in front of him, aiming straight at me.

Time slows and I freeze, doing nothing but watching the horrifying scene unfold in front of me.

Puck dives in front of me just as the knife would've impaled my stomach.

King drags me backwards.

Dax rushes to Puck.

Sandy, Mac, and Ty dive on the attacker, beating the ever-loving shit out of him.

A gunshot rings through the air; from where, I have no idea.

The attacker is left dead on the floor.

There's screaming. Loud, horrifying screams that I realise are coming from me as I stare down at Puck lying in Dax's arms, his blood covering his dirty grey jumpsuit. And suddenly, my body catches up to my brain, ten seconds too late.

"Puck! PUCK!" I scream so hard, my throat hurts.

I wriggle out of King's strong grip and drop down at Puck's side, grabbing his hands and inspecting his wound.

"Get an ambulance or something. Someone help!" I shout, looking frantically around.

But no one moves.

"KING!" I shout, but he just looks at Puck, a sadness that I've never seen shadow him before.

"It won't make a difference, Theo," Dax says calmly, putting his gun back in his belt.

"No!" I cry, holding on to Puck's hands. "Puck?" I sob into his chest, the blood from his wound coating my hair and forehead.

"T," Puck whispers, barely any life left in him.

"Don't die. Please don't die. I'm not worth dying over, Puck, please!" I wail as I take his face into both of my hands, sticky with his blood.

"Theo... it's okay," he says so, so quietly. He slowly lifts his hand from his chest and interlocks his pinkie finger with mine. "I've got you."

He smiles slightly before stilling and I watch in horror as the life leaves his eyes.

"No, Puck. Please hold me, Puck, please." I sob, the tears falling thick and fast, my finger clinging onto his tightly. A pain so strong cuts right through my chest. That should've been me and instead, Puck has once again paid the price for something that wasn't his to pay.

The prison is silent and I look up to see everyone standing around. Tears stream down grown men's faces, quiet sniffling echoing within the walls. His friends stand to my right, crying over Puck's body, limp and lifeless on the ground. Dax and King are both quiet, overwhelmed with sadness. I've never seen King so still. So devastated.

The respect pouring out of each and every single man for Puck is strong. He was their friend, their brother, their family, and everyone knew he didn't deserve to be in here.

"Theo," King says quietly, breaking the silence.

I shake my head, clinging tighter onto Puck's hand, our pinkie fingers still interlocked.

"Theo, we need to go. I don't know if there are any more threats," he whispers. Gone is the authoritative, dominant voice, but the voice of a sympathetic friend having to do the hard thing.

"I can't leave him. I can't." I cry some more.

King crouches down beside me and lifts my chin, a tear slipping out of his eye and down his cheek.

"Come on," he pleads, holding my hands and trying to pry them off of Puck's.

King hooks his baby finger into mine, detaching me from Puck and holding on to me tightly. He holds my chin with his free hand and stares directly into my eyes.

"I've got you now, sweetheart," he whispers, swiping away at the never-ending tears falling down my cheeks.

I sob uncontrollably as King lifts me into his arms and carries me away.

Away from Puck.

My friend.

My protector.

My family.

# 20.
# Theo

King cradles me in his arms through corridors and rooms I've never seen before, or maybe I have, but I never paid enough attention. My vision blurs and the rooms sway as my head continues to loll on King's shoulder. My cheeks are cold and wet, small teardrops still falling from my eyes, like the lightest of showers from the skies. You can feel it dampening your skin, but it's comforting.

King kicks open a huge, heavy door with a glowing green exit sign above it and unlike my light smattering of tears, the rain outside is hard and fast, pelting my flesh like a thousand needles injecting my skin all at once.

I take a huge breath in and roll my head off King's shoulder, letting it hang over his arm, my neck extending as my head falls back and hangs lifelessly.

Like Puck.

King picks up the pace when I hear a faint noise, like a car alarm, in the background. At least that's what I think it sounds like muffled amongst the rain.

I close my eyes and let the heavy pelts of rain and the swaying of King's strides overtake me. My arms flail out to the side, my whole body a dead weight, motionless and falling, and if it wasn't for King's hold, I would've dropped to the floor.

Suddenly, I'm thrown sideways and into the back of a car, the leather seats sliding under me as my wet body crashes onto them. I lie there, breathless, like I was in King's arms, just looking at the top of the car. The roof is matte black.

"For fuck's sake, Theo." I hear a mumble before my arms are hauled up and I'm sitting upright in the seat. King reaches across me and fastens the seat belt, slamming the door and running around the bonnet to jump into the driver's seat.

My eyes flicker around, my teeth chattering as the cold sinks in, and King mumbles something again, but I don't hear it. I just watch him fidget, trying to escape from his suit jacket.

King turns in his seat and drapes the wet blazer across me, then turns on the heat full blast and revs the engine.

My teeth finally stop chattering and my clothes are drying from the heated seats. My cheeks are still wet, but I'm no longer crying.

I'm numb.

I'm numb and broken.

And as I look out the car window and watch the raindrops race downward, I realise the sky is now crying for me because I no longer can.

We drive for what feels like hours, but I can't remember what time it was on the dash before King drove away from the huge brick building in the middle of nowhere that was my home for almost five months.

My head has stayed glued to the window the whole way, my eyes heavy but refusing to sleep, only closing every now and then to slowly blink. But I've been trying to avoid it because every time my eyes close, I see him lying on the floor, covered in his blood.

His blood that coats my hands, my hair, my clothes.

King has tried to talk to me a few times, but I never heard what he said and he gave up after so many attempts.

His jacket, now dry, still sits in the same position, draped over my front, my hands limp in my lap. On every output of breath, the window fogs, then it disappears as quickly as it arrived, only to appear again on my next breath.

The rain has let up, but the clouds are still grey, getting heavier again, ready for their next downpour and waiting for the right moment.

The car turns around a corner and it stops in front of two huge iron gates surrounded by a white brick wall on either side. Vines decorate the bars, reaching up and coiling around each one.

The gates open automatically and the car rolls forward, the gravel crunching satisfyingly underneath the tyres. The long driveway stretches down to a huge mansion, much like the white walls surrounding the place, and a large, beautiful round fountain sits in front of the grand steps leading into the house. A fountain that quite recently I'd allowed myself to remember.

A huge sigh escapes my mouth, the condensation fogging

up the whole window. The car stops outside the house, in the exact same spot my father's car had stopped all those years ago.

Up until recently, I haven't thought much about mine and King's first meeting. But since he's invaded my life once more, it's all I've thought about. That and the few occasions after before he fucked off and abandoned me.

I hate him. I hate that he's occupying my thoughts.

And I hate that he took me away from Puck.

King shuts off the engine and stills for a moment, looking into the fountain, but I keep my eyes fixed on the window, watching it fog and clear, fog and clear.

"You'll be safe here," King says, his voice deafening in the silence that's taken over the past couple hours. I jump slightly at the sound and close my eyes as tears prick my eyes once again.

After a couple minutes, his door opens and slams shut, and I peel my eyelids open to see his retreating back, making his way inside the Rhivers mansion.

His mansion.

Still, I don't move. I don't follow him or make any attempt to do anything. It's like my whole body has shut down. As I think about how badly this day has gone, there's a small tap at the window, a hesitant and sympathetic Dax outside the car. He has a small smile on his face but one of sadness. I wonder how he got here before us.

And where's Puck now?

Dax pulls on the door handle, slowly prying it open, and I find the small amount of strength I need to pull my head back up and off the window. He says nothing. Just peels off King's jacket and reaches across me to undo my seat belt. He offers me his hand, which I stare at, probably for way longer than what's deemed acceptable to stare at a hand offered to you. I gently raise my arm and grasp his hand, his palm casing mine and tightening, and I slowly move my legs outside of the car, my whole body stiff from not moving in hours. I stumble a little as I straighten up, but Dax wraps a strong arm around my back to steady me.

He slams the door behind me, but my feet still refuse to carry me forward. If I walk, I'm walking away, and I just can't do it. I look up at Dax, willing him to see my predicament, but when I meet his eyes, already understanding, I burst into tears again. He catches me in a hug so tightly, I know I'd never fall. I cry on his shoulder, soaking his shirt, taking in the comfort, though unfamiliar.

Dax's hold loosens and I grasp onto the back of his shirt, not ready to lose the support, when two strong arms circle around my waist and I sink. I turn into his arms and sink into the comfort I know. The comfort I need.

"I got you," he whispers in my ear.

He lifts me off the ground, carrying me effortlessly once again, up the steps of his grand mansion, Dax following in step beside us.

I'm so torn. The man I hate the most, the man who makes me feel like I'm anchored down, left to drown, is also my only life raft in a sea of sorrow.

How do I hate him for dragging me down when he's the only one keeping me afloat?

# 21. King

It's been a week since I brought Theo here and placed her in one of the many guest rooms. I laid her fragile body down on the bed and she instantly sank into the mattress and buried herself under the thick covers before dropping off to sleep.

Theo hasn't had this kind of comfort for months. Her body must be craving everything we all take for granted. A bed, soft pillows, a fucking duvet cover. Nice food, daylight, real people. Not criminals or men trying to assault her daily.

It's been a week. A whole week since Theo was nearly murdered. A whole week since Puck *was* murdered.

*Fuck.*

It still cuts deep to the bone that I didn't help him. I'd promised him. As soon as me and Dax figured out a way to kill my father, I promised him he'd be out of that fucking shithole. And then it just so happened that Theodora Harlow became his replacement, becoming an inmate on the day that should've been his last. I just couldn't leave her in there without protection. I couldn't. And the son of a bitch knew that as soon as she moved into the cell next door, and he didn't hesitate once to stay in and help her. Even after finding out Carlo was dead, not once did he ask to leave.

Years we've spent trying to find a way to kill Carlo Rhivers. Years making up elaborate plans and trying to find the best way to do it. Then little miss Theodora comes in and shoots him. Just shot him, in the open, in front of everyone.

Theo hasn't left the room once since I put her in there a week ago. I've tried to pry her out, letting her have the freedom of the house and the grounds, something she was deprived of back in the prison—deprived of back home—but nothing. She doesn't leave that fucking room.

I've cracked down her routine day in and day out now, silently watching her from her open doorway. She gets out of bed close to noon, spends up to an hour, no less, in the shower, then changes into lounge clothes I left for her, just to spend the rest of the day sleeping or staring out the window.

I know life has been hard for her the past five months, and I know she's hurting over Puck. We all are. Hell, I've known him since I was a kid. But in this life, our world, we can't just sit and grieve. We have to keep going.

*I* have to keep going.

I MAKE my way through Theo's room, not bothering to knock. I've left it unlocked for days now, letting her know she's free to leave the room, but still, she doesn't.

Unsurprisingly, she's lying on the bed, staring out the window, her face bored, and my restraint snaps.

"Move!" I say, losing my last shred of patience.

She turns to look at me but does nothing.

"Fucking. Move," I almost shout, stepping up to the bed and towering over her. She looks into my eyes, but I can't read her. I have no idea what she's thinking. And that's one of the things I hate the most.

"This is ridiculous. You can't fucking stay in here forever, Theodora!"

"Why not?" she says, almost casually. Is she kidding me?

"You can't spend the rest of your life lying in this goddamn bed."

"What can I do, King, huh?" she starts off quietly. "Walk around your fancy fucking house? Take a stroll through the gardens? Bake a cake in your no doubt massive fucking kitchen?" She's shouting now, sitting up in the bed, stabbing her finger right into my chest. "I'm your fucking prisoner, King. Let's not pretend anything's changed."

"If you were my prisoner, Theodora, do you think I would've left the door unlocked? Do you think I would've left you to your own devices?"

She scoffs then.

"Oh, come off it, King. If I walked out this door, I'd have you or some beefy bodyguard following me around. There's no fucking freedom in that. I'm your fucking prisoner and you fucking know it!" she sasses. And unfortunately for her, she picked the wrong day to start a fight with me.

"Fine, if that's what you want to be, that's how you can be treated." I grab her wrist quickly, still poking into my chest, and yank her up roughly, her arm close to being pulled out of the socket.

"King!" she screams, trying to resist my pull. But I'm stronger.

I throw her over my shoulder, gripping her thighs harshly as she pounds my back. We've been in this position too many times.

"Fucking put me down!"

I ignore her request and carry her through the mansion, yanking on the handle of the door so forcefully, it almost breaks off its hinges. I make my way down the steep stairs, plunging into the darkness, illuminated just slightly from a small window at the far end of the room.

I walk into the cell, buried deep under the Rhivers mansion, and throw Theo on her ass right in the middle, turning my back on her and slamming the huge cell gate shut, the lock clicking into place automatically.

She jumps up onto her bare feet and runs at the bars, trying to grab at me through them.

"What the fuck, King?!" she shouts, panic lacing her tone as she comes to terms with what's happening.

"This is what you wanted right, Theodora?" I snarl. "Well, now you are my fucking prisoner." I spit at the floor in front of her and see the hurt and anger flash through her eyes before I turn my back on her and leave her there.

"WHERE'S THEO?" Dax asks, an eyebrow raised at me in questioning.

"In the cell," Rori says, laughing slightly at Dax's horrified look.

I'm in my office, catching up on everything I've missed recently and checking back payments from the other two

Districts. Not long ago, Rori walked in, perched her tiny ass on my armchair and opened up her laptop and started working, ignoring my withering glare in her direction.

She and Dax have been together a few years now and are consumed by each other. He found her broken and he saved her. They are it for each other. Only the little shit likes to be a massive pain in my ass and walks around my house like she's the one who owns the place. Strutting into my office whilst I'm working to do her own shit on her laptop. I gave her her own office for this purpose. Not that she ever uses it.

"Why the fuck is she in the cell?" he questions, looking shocked and maybe slightly angry? I don't know. His face is hard to read.

"She wants to be a prisoner, she can be a fucking prisoner," I justify, shrugging my shoulders.

Rori's high-pitched laugh bursts out of her lungs, the long, silvery plait falling off her shoulder as her head rolls back off the chair.

"Fuck off, Aurora," I spit.

She turns to look at me, her eyebrows raised and a challenge in her eyes.

"I mean it... get the fuck out!" I shout, pointing to the door.

She flinches slightly but then maintains her composure, never one to back down from anyone.

"Put away your umbrella, King. I don't need your shade," she fires back with an eye roll, tucking her laptop under her arm. She swiftly gives Dax a soft kiss as she passes and opens the door. She stops in the open doorway and looks from me to the door and then back to me before putting her middle finger up and smirking, leaving the door wide-fucking-open in her wake.

Dax huffs out a laugh at her pettiness before closing the door and coming back to the middle of the room, occupying Rori's now vacant seat.

"King," he says, trying to retrieve the answers from me.

"I'm not leaving her in there. It's just for the day. She was being a little bitch."

Dax lets out a short laugh, then clears his throat.

"Of course she was. She's been holed up in that prison for five months, then she lost her only friend, and now she's been dragged here by a nutcase who can't decide how he feels."

I look up at him to find him giving me a judgemental stare. I return the look, throwing daggers his way. I know how I feel, don't I?

"Why would she leave her room?" he continues, staring me down. "She's lost, confused, heartbroken, and grieving. You can't blame the girl."

"Since when did you become so noble?" I mock.

Dax rolls his eyes.

"You know I'm right, man. Just fucking treat her like a human being. It'll make shit easier for you both."

I roll my eyes at that.

"Anyway." I cough, changing the subject. "I've been trying to get in touch with Kennedy to book our meeting, but I can't get a hold of him. He's been in the Third District a couple of times this week, so not sure what business he's doing, but we need to find out alongside getting our money, finding out who set the attack on Theo and finding that anonymous fucker who gave Kennedy all that cash."

Dax nods and taps away at his phone.

"I'll see what I can find out about why he was in the Third. I'll get Rori on CCTV checks," he replies, standing up promptly to get to work. I nod back, always appreciative of him. And Rori.

The girl is a liability, but she's loyal and works hard, and whether I like it or not, I love her like a sister. Like Bonnie.

I sigh and shut down my computer before standing and twirling the key to Theo's cell around my finger. Let's go and ignite the little firecracker some more, shall we?

## 22.
## Theo

The waterfall crashes loudly against the rocks and the surface below, the sound deafening as the engine of King's bike quietens. I look out in awe at the huge mass of blue reflective water cascading in a beautiful chaos.

It's hidden way deep in the woods surrounding the Three Districts, possibly even crossing onto Newlands territory. I never knew about it. King gets off the bike and holds his hand out to me, and I look at him hesitantly.

"It's okay, we won't get caught. No one comes here," he says with certainty. When I hesitate a second longer, he smiles. "I promise. I won't let you get caught."

Well, I've snuck out this far. What's the point in not going that little bit further?

Me and King have been speaking for a month now, ever since that day I met him at his mansion. I had a letter arrive the next day with my name on the envelope in scrawny handwriting. I've never received a letter before.

Inside was a small ripped piece of paper with a phone number written on it and a single sentence.

## I said I'd see you again...
## King

Did I have doubts that this is some sort of set-up? Of course. But I take the plunge anyway because in those few minutes with King, it was the most I've felt in all my life. I want that feeling again. We spoke for hours on the phone day and night during that month, but finally we found a time we could sneak out and see each other.

And that's how I find myself turning in for the night early, locking my door, climbing out the window, and hiding in the bushes until Emerson walks around the corner. I take off down the driveway and wait until King appears, then climb onto the back of his bike, trusting him with everything I have, because what have I really got to lose?

"It's beautiful," I whisper in awe as he takes my hand, leading me towards the edge of the rocks. A current of electricity shoots through my arm and around my whole body, lighting me up at the contact. Romance has always been fictional to me. But now I'm beginning to understand where authors get their inspiration from. It feels different, like some sort of special.

King helps me climb up a few more rocks until we're a quarter of the way up the waterfall, staring into the deep blue water rippling below. He smiles. The biggest smile I think I've ever seen.

Memories of our texts and phone calls float around my head. The pointless conversations about TV shows and books (on my part anyway, King doesn't really read), to deeper conversations, like how I have zero freedom and *the business trips I'm forced to sometimes take with my father. Or how he's next in line to rule the First District. He tells me about his cousin Dax, who I've only seen in pictures, and I tell him about my mother, who's my best friend.*

*It's been the most wonderful month and I finally feel like my life is starting to begin. Meeting boys and having crushes should've been something I experienced years ago, not at the age of sixteen. But I do have a crush. A big one. And I don't think I'll ever feel about anyone else like I do King. He's shown me there's more out there. That there's more to life than being a prisoner in your own home.*

"Ready?" King asks, grinning more mischievously now as he wraps his hands around the bottom of his T-shirt and pulls it up over his head.

I blush at the view. A lot.

King's smile grows even bigger as he notices the pink shade coating my cheeks. Hell, he can probably hear my heartbeat banging on the outside of my chest. I don't know where to look, my gaze flickering from his eyes to his toned chest, to a solid six-pack. A six-pack? He's seventeen! How has he got a six-pack this good?

As if the heat of my gaze is burning his skin, I notice the bulge growing in his shorts and my cheeks redden even more. What is happening?

"My eyes are up here, sweetheart." He winks as I quickly find eye contact, embarrassment flooding my veins that I've been caught staring not only at his abs but at his semi-hard dick.

Trying to play it off cool, I reply, "And your dick is down there."

*I shrug, like it's absolutely no big deal, but inside I'm dying.*

*I can't believe I just said that.*

*I notice the slightest shadow of pink on his cheeks and I dance in victory internally that I got a reaction out of him. Then he laughs. A loud belly laugh and I swear it's the most beautiful sound I've ever heard, echoing with the waterfall.*

"Smooth. Real smooth."

*I laugh too. I can't help it. He's infectious.*

*King steps up closer to me and slowly peels my T-shirt from my body, leaving me in my plain black T-shirt bra and shorts. I fidget, slightly uncomfortable under his wandering gaze, but his eyes are filled with anything but judgement.*

"Ready?" *he asks, grabbing hold of my hand and walking us right to the edge of the rocks.*

*I look up at him, amused, nervous, and excited all at once, but I've no idea if it's because of jumping or because of him.*

"Ready!" *I smile and turn to face the water.*

*He squeezes my hand tighter and after silently counting to three in my head, I follow his lead and we jump off. Floating in the air for mere seconds, free as a bird with no other feeling than pure joy before crash landing into the depths of the water, my hand losing King's as we go under.*

*I take in the peacefulness at the bottom, opening my eyes to see the sandy gravel floor and small fishes swimming away from the interruption. A smile pulls at my lips whilst I continue to hold my breath and I push up from the ground, making my way to the surface.*

*As I appear above the water, I take a deep breath in and stroke the hair back from my face. I scan the surface for King when strong arms wrap around my stomach from behind, a* solid body holding on to me, feelings I've never felt before overtaking my emotions and senses.

I turn in his arms and take him in. His hair is everywhere, darker than normal with the water. Small water droplets gently slide down his face, off his nose, and glisten on his eyelashes. He's beautiful.

One of his hands leaves my back and he cups my cheek, holding me close, our lips inches apart. I try to steady my breathing.

"Are you okay?" he whispers, but loud enough for me to hear him over the waterfall.

"Yes," I whisper back.

And he kisses me.

King parts his lips and places them perfectly on mine, stealing my breath away and giving me his. Our lips move in perfect harmony. His tongue rolls along my bottom lip before I open up further for him, allowing him entrance, and all I feel is pure bliss.

True, I've never been kissed before, but they can't all be like this, can they?

After the most passionate moment of my life passes too soon, we both pull back to catch our breath and I can't stop smiling. The tingling of his lips still on mine.

King reaches his thumb across and rubs it gently on my lower lip, and even though it was the quietest of whispers and the waterfall was so loud I could have imagined it, I heard the words like they were whispered right to my soul.

"Don't go anywhere."

Okay, I promised.

"Wake the fuck up." King's voice wakes me and I scrunch up my eyes, trying to clear my head from my dream of a pinnacle moment in my life, before King fucked up that girl who believed in some sort of love.

"Wake. The. Fuck. Up!" he says louder, and I roll my eyes.

I turn onto my back on the concrete floor and look over at the gate. He's standing tall on the other side, his arms crossed in front of him, a scowl on his face.

I shift a little, leaning onto my elbows, studying him. Gone is the boy who kissed me at the waterfall. Gone is the boy who promised an expectation that was tarnished. Instead is a man, almost nine years later, who's completely unrecognisable. A man who runs the First District, his father's son through and through.

I hate how he makes me feel. How I still long for the boy from all those years ago.

"Enjoying your cell?" He smirks, raising a brow.

I look around the small square box I'm in. Just me and the concrete walls. No mattress, no toilet. Though the conditions are actually worse than my cell at the prison, the daylight that shone through the small window was a luxury I didn't have back there. But the sun settled hours ago and now it's almost pitch-black, just a few rays from the moon sparing light into some of the cell. Half of King's frame is illuminated by the white glow.

"Why, wanna join me?" I tease. However, the disgust is

apparent in my tone. He rolls his eyes at my sarcasm, the disgust also shining in his eyes.

I jump up onto my feet and stalk over to the bars. Gripping them, I cock my head at him, taking him in again, my dream playing on my mind.

Is the King that I knew when we were teenagers still a part of him? Puck seemed to respect him. And the way he carried me out of that prison after what happened to Puck, that wasn't the same King who's standing before me now.

I narrow my eyes, the confusion weighing heavily on my shoulders.

"What?" he questions when I just continue to stare at him.

I look into his eyes and see the boy from my dream, hear the whisper light in my ears.

"Don't go anywhere," I whisper, looking at his lips.

He takes a slow step closer.

"What?"

"You said don't go anywhere," I say a little bit louder. "But then you—"

Before I can continue, King's hand reaches out and clasps my throat, and I claw at his hand through the bars, trying to alleviate the pressure on my neck, but his hand is too big and too strong. He's squeezing so tightly that I'm gasping for breath.

Anger flashes through King's eyes as he watches me try to catch any ounce of air that I can force into my lungs. My eyes water and I dig my nails into his hand harshly. Something seems to click into place and King releases his hold on my throat. I stumble back, falling onto my knees and rubbing at my neck to ease the slight pain that's lingering. But I never take my eyes off King.

He runs his hands over his face, shaking himself out of whatever emotion took hold of him, and I see him.

The boy.

The boy from the waterfall.

A lone tear drips down my cheek for that boy. What happened to him?

King pulls a key out of his pocket and unlocks the gate. I sit back on my heels and glance up at him as he walks towards me. He bends down, bringing his hand up to my cheek, and wipes the tear away with his thumb before trailing his hand down to my neck, gently stroking it, replacing the harsh grip with a soft caress.

He trails his hand across my shoulder and places his hand in mine, pulling me up to my feet. On shaky legs, I stand awkwardly straight and his hand leaves mine and cups my face again. I sigh into it slightly, his face moving closer and closer until our lips are inches apart.

"Are you okay?" he whispers.

I laugh slightly, although nothing about this is funny. How have we come full circle? I nod slowly, then look into his eyes.

"Yes," I breathe out quietly. His lips capture mine, and the same overwhelming feelings flood my veins again, the feelings of a child almost in love wrack my body.

I melt into him, wrapping my arms tightly around his neck, clinging onto him like the life raft he is. He ravages my mouth, his tongue demanding entrance regardless of permission. It battles with mine, a hunger so eager in both of us.

King's arms unravel and slide down my body, cupping

my ass and giving it a hard squeeze. Pulling away from the kiss, he bites my bottom lip, dragging it out, and as he lets it go, he bends his knees and commands, "Jump."

AND I DO. I pounce off the floor and his arms flex under my ass, lifting me, and I wrap my legs tightly around his waist. He walks us to the back of the cell, shrouding us in darkness, and slams my back against the cold brick wall. A gasp, filled with pleasure and shock, escapes my lips.

King growls and captures my lips again, the bulge in his pants growing bigger and bigger every second. Needing more, I grind my hips against his shaft, but there are too many layers between us.

"King," I whimper, needing something more. Needing him.

Suddenly, King's lips fall away from mine and he slams me back down to my feet, only just catching myself before I fall. He shrugs out of his blazer faster than lightning, then reaches behind him and pulls out a sharp blade from his belt. In one swift motion, never breaking his eyes away from me, he tears my T-shirt over my head, pulls down my shorts, and cuts through my underwear with his knife so I'm completely bare to him.

Then he's down on his knees, tossing the knife aside and devouring my pussy before I can even think straight.

"Oh fuck," I whimper as his tongue caresses my clit. King lifts my left leg and rests it over his shoulder, giving him more access, and without a moment of hesitation, he slides two fingers into me expertly, curling them and hitting that spot with such skill, I see stars.

My mind struggles to comprehend what's happening. The remnants of my dream are floating around my head, reminding me of how young we were but how I thought he was it for me. Then he abandoned me, and years later I found myself in his clutches again, like time hadn't gotten in the way.

I grab fistfuls of his hair, watching his face buried between my thighs and feeling his fingers expertly move around my walls.

His tongue teases my clit and the pressure building from his fingers is overpowering and my knees begin to buckle.

"King, I'm gonna come," I breathe out.

Just as my orgasm crests, King pulls his fingers out and replaces them with his tongue, flicking my clit instead with his thumb, and I lose complete control. King swallows my orgasm, licking up every inch of me as his tongue devours my pussy.

A breathless moment later, King slides his tongue out and up my slit, and my clit twitches, sensitive after the orgasm I just had. He licks up my body, past my navel, over each nipple, suckling my neck before kissing me, sharing my taste with me, and he moans in my mouth as I take it all.

My hands find some strength and I rub over his dick. Grabbing his belt buckle, I undo it with shaky fingers. I finally get it free, yank down his slacks, and hold him tightly in my hand, sizing him up and marvelling at how my small hand has so much space to play.

I stroke up and down his dick, rolling my thumb over the tip and wiping at the bead of pre-cum leaking out the top. I bring my thumb up to my mouth, rubbing it over my lips, and taste his arousal. It's the final straw.

King hikes up my left leg to his hip and holds it there under my thigh, squeezing with just the right amount of pressure. He grabs hold of his dick and lines it up to my entrance before cursing.

"Fuck, let me get a condom."

"No," I almost shout, grabbing his dick and lining it back up to me. "I want you. No barriers between us."

He looks at me and I smile.

"I'm good," I reassure him, and it's enough for him.

He pushes up into me and my back slams against the wall. He stretches me wide, and I scream in pain and pleasure, trying to adjust to the feeling. It's only my second time and I wasn't prepared. But King draws in and out slowly, letting me get accustomed to his size, when his fingers find my clit.

His thrusts get harder and deeper with each flick of my clit, and I grind with him, taking him deeper.

He removes his fingers, then whispers, "Touch yourself."

My hand replaces his, rubbing circles against my clit. With one hand still supporting my thigh, King brings his other hand up to my neck, forcing my head back up against the wall.

This is a position we've been in many times and it feels right. It feels like *us*. His hand fits perfectly on my throat, and his fingers fit like a glove as they wrap right around, able to crush and cut off my air supply at any second.

My breathing becomes more rapid as I struggle for breath and my moans turn to screams as he fucks me hard. With each thrust, my body slams up against the wall and his dick hits that spot deep inside.

Another orgasm is threatening as my fingers move faster on my clit to match his pace.

"Let that pretty tight pussy come all over my dick, sweetheart," King rasps and I lose it again. My second orgasm bursts through every cell in my body, having complete control over all of my senses.

King grunts and curses, and I faintly hear him moan, "Finally," as he releases his load inside me, filling me up with every last drop, never faltering his pace until he's completely emptied himself inside me. He stills and we freeze for a moment in time, his dick twitching deep inside my core, his hand still wrapped firmly around my throat.

Our breathing slows whilst we take in what just happened and I stare at this man King has become.

He's no longer that boy from the waterfall, but he's neither the man who made me his prisoner. Somewhere in between all of that is the real King and fuck knows what journey I'll end up on to find him.

## 23.
## Theo

Not two minutes later, I'm back on my bare ass on the floor, watching King's retreating back as he leaves me again. He doesn't look back as he turns out of the cell, leaving the door wide-open.

His actions are clear. He knows what just happened shouldn't have, but he's not locking me in here either. The open cell is my choice to leave. I curl myself up, bringing my legs up to my chest, and hug them close.

It seems ridiculous to find comfort within four brick walls, but it's safe. I know how this works. Out there, in the Rhivers mansion, everything is so unknown to me that the thought of being out of my comfort zone petrifies me.

Sleeping in that ginormous bed should've felt like home, but to be honest, I've never craved my shitty mattress back in the prison more in my life. Sure, my new bed was comfortable and heavenly, but I don't deserve it.

I'm struggling with my emotions. Losing Puck brought on many feelings I'd long since buried. I'd never experienced grief before my mother died and I didn't think I would again as I have no one close to me who could hurt me so much.

Until Puck.

I murdered Carlo Rhivers for revenge and peace of mind. Instead, I got my heart bandaged up to be ripped to shreds by grief and anger.

Wrapped up in my thoughts once again, I look around the four brick walls bathed in darkness. A shiver runs down my spine to the tip of my toes, and I weakly go to collect my clothes from the ground.

My legs ache as I pull my shorts up and I wobble slightly. My mind is trying to play catch-up on memories of my mother, Puck, and King all at once. I take in the small cell and replay what happened only moments ago, from teasing him to seeing him leave my ass on the cold floor.

Why would he just leave me? After everything? After fucking me up against this goddamn wall, he just drops my ass and leaves. Like I'm a quick fuck. I mean, that's what it was, I suppose. I know better than to think King is capable of anything regarding feelings for himself or other people.

The hurt I felt momentarily is replaced by anger. I'm angry that he left me. I'm angry that I actually care that he left me. Fuck this.

Now dressed, I charge through the open door and turn the corner to find the steep steps that King carried me down this morning now bathed in shadows. I tentatively step onto the first one, a low creak echoing on each step that I take whilst I use the wall to feel against to help keep my balance.

Reaching the top, I place my hand gently on the round doorknob and turn it quickly before I can talk myself out of it and run back to the cell. The room instantly brightens in a warm white glow and I squint my eyes against it, letting them adjust to the light.

After blinking a few times, I fully open my eyes, close

the door, and lean against it to find myself in a long hallway. I look left and right, but it's deserted and there's no sign of life anywhere.

Taking a deep breath, I push away from the door and head to the right slowly. The walls are cream, the carpet a soft black under my feet, and spread out evenly along the walls are large gold photo frames, bringing colour into the hallway, of people I don't recognise. Men, women, families. I'm assuming they are generations of the Rhivers family.

Walking down this clean corridor, my bare feet on the carpet, I've never felt so dirty. Unlike the pristine white walls and floors of my home, or should I say, my father's home, already from this small hallway I can tell there's more colour and life and stories to be told hidden within the walls of the Rhivers mansion.

I come to a halt at the end of the corridor to a portrait of people I do recognise. Carlo Rhivers sits in a large chair in the middle of the frame. His wife, Emily Rhivers, stands next to him, her body turned into his side as her arm rests lightly on his shoulder. Behind him are two men, one who I recognise to be Edison Ramon, leader of the Third District. The man next to him looks familiar, but I can't put a name to him, but similarities between him and Ramon are there. Maybe relatives? And finally on Carlo's right-hand side are two faces I know very well. My mother and father stand next to Carlo, Kennedy's hand around Elisa's waist, small smiles coming from both of them.

I study my parents and wonder when this could have been taken. King's mum, Emily, died when he was four, so this was over twenty-two years ago. I wonder why they had this photo taken. It was clearly a District Leader's family portrait. Maybe the man with Edison Ramon is his partner?

After being distracted for far too long, I leave the portrait and make a mental note to come back to it.

I take a left at the end of the hallway, and after minutes of making my way through the mansion, a wide-open entryway greets me, the same cream walls and black carpet, but there's a huge dual staircase, with golden bannisters and a golden chandelier hanging right down the middle. It's beautiful.

I'm not completely blind to a beautiful house. I lived in one myself, but the Rhivers mansion is extraordinary in comparison.

Quiet chatter comes from downstairs and I continue cautiously down them. Even amongst the beauty, my anger still simmers just below the surface. I can't believe King just left me to find my way around.

As I reach the bottom of the stairs, I notice some guards positioned near the large doors on either side of the foyer. I make eye contact with one and he slowly juts his head to the left and gives me a small wink. I return his helpfulness with a small smile and make my way to the left, hoping to find someone. There are more doors and more extravagant art on the walls, but I hesitate just before the open doorway to the room where the light conversation is coming from.

I take a deep breath to steady my nerves and rein in my anger before I go all guns blazing and step forward, making my presence known in the doorway.

The conversation halts immediately as I scan over the faces within. Two I know very well and one not at all. King is sitting on the right-hand side of the table, knife and fork in hand as he's tucking into his food. He barely glances my way before dismissing me and returning back to his plate.

On the opposite side of the table is Dax, relaxed in his chair with a small smile on his face in greeting. His hands are rubbing small circles on the legs that are placed in his lap.

I follow the owner's legs up their body until my eyes land on hers. Slouched in her chair is a gorgeous, dainty girl with shiny, almost silver hair, trussed up into two long, thick plaits. She doesn't smile at me, just lazily looks over her shoulder, no emotion on her face.

"Come and sit, Theodora. There's a place for you," King says calmly.

My eyes scan back to his and I narrow them at his audacity to just act like nothing happened between us.

I stalk through the room and see what I'm assuming is my plate, filled with a pasta dish that looks delicious, but my mouth is dry and I seem to have lost my appetite.

I look at King, who conveniently is sat next to me, and I scoff before dropping into the seat.

"It's good to see you up and about, Theo," Dax's soft voice says through the quiet, and I look at him and smile gently. He's always been nice to me. He doesn't deserve the backlash like his cousin does.

"This is Rori," he says, squeezing the girl's leg.

I turn my gaze to her and try to keep that same smile on my face, but the lack of emotion on her part is making me slightly uncomfortable.

"Hi, I'm Theo," I squeak, quickly clearing my throat and cringing at my lack of communication skills.

"I know," she says, a raspy yet sweet voice penetrating the air.

Dax rolls his eyes at her lack of response but honestly, I'd rather she didn't pretend around me. By the looks of things, Rori is Dax's and Dax is Rori's. The possessive hand she now has on his arm is clear as day. She knows these men and this house. I am merely an intruder.

"So how long do you intend to stay?" she says again, her tone strong, biting a tube of pasta off her fork. I open my mouth to respond, not even entirely sure of my answer, before King speaks for me.

"Until the prison is safe for her to go back to."

Everyone's head jerks to King, all with similar facial expressions of confusion. King looks up and takes his turn to look at us all individually.

"What?" he questions casually, shoving a piece of pasta in his mouth.

"Since when were we sending her back to the prison?" Dax asks, obviously completely out of the loop with King.

"Since I decided about half an hour ago." King shrugs.

My heart drops and my anger boils as I know exactly what he's referring to. What, he fucks me and then wants to send me back just like that? I go to say just that before a harsh laugh pierces through the room and my daggers land on Rori.

Everyone turns to look at her as her laugh comes to a halt.

"God, King, you're such a dick," she says, laughter still in her voice.

Now I'm startled again. Is she defending me?

"Excuse me?" King replies sternly, clearly not impressed with Rori calling him a dick.

"Don't *excuse me*, King," Rori mocks. "You're gonna fuck

the girl, then just send her back to the prison like some criminal booty call?" She laughs again with a shake of her head.

I'm dumbstruck. How does she know we fucked? Is she defending me or not? I can't make out what point she's trying to make. A criminal booty call. I feel offended, but I'm not sure if she meant to offend. Jesus, who is this girl?

"Watch your mouth, Aurora," King spits at her.

"Why? Because I'm right?" Rori, or Aurora apparently, fires back. "The girl has been locked up in your stupid little prison for months for you to drag her here, get in her knickers, and send her back because you're scared of your feelings. How petty."

Scared of his feelings?

"Ror," Dax warns under his breath and turns Rori's face in his hand to look at him.

My brain is overloading and before my mouth can catch up, I let out a, "Umm."

And all three heads now turn back to me.

King looks furious, Dax looks like he's slipping, keeping himself calm, and Rori seems bored.

"I have no idea if you're defending me or not," I say, talking to Rori as she raises an eyebrow. I turn my head to King and finish. "But wherever you put me, I don't give a fuck. I'm in fucking hell regardless, and even more so around you. Please, send me back to my cell. I'd much prefer it."

King looks surprised at my outburst.

"I can easily send you back downstairs, Theodora."

"No, I said *my* cell." I stand, pushing my chair back. "My cell at that shitty prison of yours. Where I had friends, where I knew what to expect, where *you* weren't around."

"You don't have friends there anymore, Theodora." King

disregards me and the wound is peeled wide-open, cutting me deep at the reminder.

"I-I..." I stutter, trying to get the words out.

"Sit down," he finalises, dismissing any more of my rant.

Feeling defeated and cut open, I slowly go to take my seat, but Rori slams her feet to the ground and pushes her chair back, snapping my attention over to her.

"Fuck off, King. Do you not have a sensitive bone in your body?"

Now this time I know for sure she's defending me. Whether it was my vulnerability and my lack of strength to keep fighting back that did it, or she's just had enough, I don't know, but I'm grateful.

"I don't need to be sensitive," he mumbles and it almost looks like he's cowering under Rori's presence. Her loud, sarcastic laugh echoes through the room again.

"I'll be sure to throw the loss of Puck in your face next time I wanna knock you down. Maybe Bonnie, hmm?" she spits, literal venom coming out of her mouth.

I wince at Bonnie's name. I spoke to Puck many times about her but never with King. I forget he was her brother and I feel bad for never mentioning her.

"Rori," Dax warns again, standing up too.

Rori huffs and walks to the door, halting at the entrance. She turns around to look me dead in the eyes.

"You coming?" she asks, and although I have no idea who she is or whether she even likes me, going with her seems a better deal than staying here.

I jump up and spin on my heel as I make my way to the door, but before I even get two steps in, King's large hand wraps around my wrist, holding me back.

"You will sit and eat, Theodora. You haven't eaten in ages. You're weak," he fires at me, a tone so commanding that it knocks me for six.

Rori sighs and as I look back at her, the doorway is empty, and Dax is following her out of it. I roll my eyes at everyone's defeat, including my own.

Showing no signs of movement, King drags me backwards and forces me back into my chair.

"You fucking move, I'll tie you to it."

I stare at my plate and consider running, up for the challenge. But I know he'd do it. Rori leaving proves exactly that. No one was going to win here apart from him.

I think about what he said over and over again in my head.

*"You're weak."*

I know he's referring to the fact I haven't eaten, but I *am* weak. What happened to Theodora Harlow? The same one who killed the big, bad Carlo Rhivers five months ago?

"Theodora, eat!" King demands again but quieter.

"I don't want to," I whisper.

"Quite frankly, I don't give a fuck. Eat your goddamn food and be grateful."

"Grateful?" I question, finally looking up at him. "You want me to be grateful?"

King rolls his eyes, preparing for yet another argument.

"Sure, okay, thank you, King, for keeping me alive and safe under your roof, but don't you dare ask me to be grateful for *anything* else. What am I so lucky about, huh? My dad disowning me? Losing Puck? Your shitty treatment of me? How about being fucked like a goddamn whore and then dropped on my ass when you got your bit?"

"Theodora, let's not forget why the fuck you're here in the first place!" he throws back at me. I stand, completely losing my shit.

"Fuck Carlo. You didn't even like Carlo! Don't throw that in my face. You have fucking everything, King. Everything! And what do I have—"

"Everything?" King interrupts, standing to tower over me. "No, Theo, I don't have everything. I have Dax, and Rori, and you. That's it!" he shouts, locking my eyes with his.

I recoil slightly, taking a step back away from him. My heart thumps in my chest at his revelation.

*I have Dax, and Rori, and you.*

*You.*

My eyes water as I think of mine and King's rocky relationship since we were teens. He doesn't have me at all.

"You're wrong, King," I whisper. A tear drops onto my cheek and King's eyes follow it immediately. "You don't have me. You lost that right when you left me nine years ago."

I don't wait around and I know he's lost his fight. Just as I make it to the door, his voice stops me.

"Nine years ago? You're holding what happened between us as kids against me?" His voice is quiet and he sounds genuinely confused.

"I was. And I can see nothing's changed. You just use people for your own gain and then dispose of them. Lucky for me, it's happened twice." I scoff and leave the room.

## 24. King

It's been two months since me and Theo snuck out to the waterfall. It's not often that we're able to sneak out, but when we do, it's like everything in my life doesn't matter.

Instead of growing up, going to school, and having a bunch of friends to get up to no good with and talk to girls, I had a completely different upbringing. Sure, I was Carlo Rhivers son and the heir to the First District. And I had my cousin Dax, who was also my best friend, and Puck, the maid's son. But that was it.

Meeting Theo was like a breath of fresh air and it felt good to feel something for someone.

I'm sitting in the games room with Puck, playing a game of pool and thinking about where we could go tonight. I'm seeing her and can't wait to kiss her again.

My phone vibrates with a new message, Theo's reply to my last one.

**Haha, you wish King ;) but maybe later? I can't wait to see you! x**

*I laugh at her teasing and go to type back a message when I hear a throat clear.*

*"You gonna play or shall I take your shot?" Puck asks, amused.*

*I roll my eyes and put my phone in my pocket.*

*"You make me sick." Puck laughs, pointing at my pocket.*

*"Oh yeah, Pucker, like you're any better with Bonnie?" I laugh, calling him out on his shit.*

*Puck and Bonnie have been together for nearly two years. At first, I was very protective of Bonnie. It's bad enough that she's been hidden from the whole world and completely secluded. I didn't need Puck coming in and making matters worse. Especially because he was sixteen and Bonnie only fourteen when they got together. At first, it was just innocent crushes, but now, even still so young at eighteen, you can tell Puck loves her.*

*I love my sister and will do anything I can to protect her. Aside from living in seclusion, growing up without a mother had a huge impact on her and I noticed Bonnie struggle more and more each day. Puck came at the right time for her.*

*Thinking about my mother still hurts. She died of an overdose, leaving me and Bonnie in the care of father dearest. It hurts that she left us, that she didn't try harder. And I don't even know what was so hard for her that she couldn't live this life anymore.*

*After scrambling my thoughts and playing another round, the door to the room is slammed open and almost knocked off its hinges. My father storms in and grabs Puck by the collar, spitting and shouting in his face. I'm hauled back by a guard who followed Carlo in.*

"What the fuck, Dad?" I shout, trying to make sense of the situation.

"This will be the last time I ever fucking see your face again. Stay away from my child," Carlo shouts, punching Puck square in the jaw. Two more men come in and haul Puck's writhing body out of the room as he fights for freedom.

At first, I thought Carlo was talking about me. Stay away from my child. But he must mean Bonnie. He doesn't have it in him to say daughter.

My father has never come to terms with the fact my mother had Bonnie. A beautiful little girl. No, he wanted sons for heirs. A daughter was just unacceptable to him. Hence why he kept her hidden away. The shame, apparently, was too much to cope with.

"King, KING!" Puck shouts as he tries to reach out for me. I push against the guard holding me, trying to get to him, but it's no use.

"Tell Bonnie I love her!" he shouts and I start to panic big time.

What the FUCK is going on?

Carlo laughs loudly as Puck gets dragged one way and I the other. I keep fighting against the guard, but suddenly everything goes black as I'm knocked out.

I wake up in my room with a banging headache, but I'm not sure if that's because of the concussion or trying to make sense of everything that happened. All I know is I need to get to Bonnie to check that she's okay and find out where they've taken Puck. And where the fuck is Dax?

Approaching my door, I breathe a sigh of relief to find it's unlocked and quietly make my way through the house, attempting to get to Bonnie's room first. Before I can go any *further, I hear a gunshot. Loud and clear ringing through the house, coming from the cells downstairs.*

*I run. I run faster than I ever have in my life, bombarded by thoughts of Puck being tied up down there and dead on the floor. But why? Why would they do that to him?*

*Coming up to the end of the hallway, I freeze, halting in front of a portrait of the District families. Voices are travelling up the stairs from the cells and I strain my ears to hear the conversation.*

"Right, now that that's dealt with, let's get one thing straight. No one knew about her anyway apart from the people on the grounds. We'll tell a story about some tragic accident. King will come around. Puck is dealt with and no one will ever hear about the pregnancy. Understood?"

*I hear mumbles coming from the people around him, but the words that just came out of my father's mouth are swirling a mile a minute around my head.*

*No one knew about her. Puck's dealt with. Pregnancy. What the fuck?*

*Carlo and four men appear from the doorway and my father hands his gun over to one of them.*

"Now clean this and take it away before anyone sees. And someone bury her body discreetly, for Christ's sake." *The words fly from Carlo's mouth so casually.*

*My heart stops.*

*My world stops.*

*Has Carlo just murdered Bonnie? My sister? His own daughter?*

*Carlo turns from his men and halts in his steps, locking eyes with me, a look of murder shadowing his features. Although that could have already been there before.*

"King. Haven't I told you to never eavesdrop on a conversation not meant for you to hear? There will always be consequences, Son."

I see red. A huge tidal wave of anger courses through each and every vein, and I charge at him.

Two men come forward and hold me back as I fight and rage at my father.

"How fucking dare you. You murderer. How could you?" I yell, tears falling from my eyes.

"Grow up, King," Carlo spits.

"She was your daughter. MY SISTER!"

"She was no child of mine. Getting herself knocked up by the help's son no less. She deserved it. So did he," my father replies so calmly, like this isn't a big deal.

"I'll make you pay for this!" I shout back. He will never get away with this.

"You will tell no one, King." He looks me dead in the eyes, a sudden threat lacing his tone.

"Try me," I challenge. I will avenge my sister and Puck.

My father holds my stare for a beat, thinking over his options. I'm sure he'd happily kill me right now, but then there'd be no heir to his stupid District and that is more important to him than anything.

"He can have the same fate as Puck."

He dismisses me and walks away, the two guards dragging me down the hallway before I'm knocked out again on the back of my head.

## PRISONER

I WAKE up in a small room. Four walls box me in and the lighting is dark and murky. I look up and find a large, metal, barred gate closing me in, with Puck leaning on it, watching me. I try to make sense of what's going on before he speaks up.

"Some sort of prison, mate. Fuck knows who's in here, but it's some sort of secret organisation the Districts have been working on."

I look up at him and see the look of defeat in his eyes. I'm glad to see him alive, but then my heart shatters as I remember the events of the last, what, twelve hours maybe? Who knows.

"They killed her, man," I whisper, my eyes filling to the brim before overflowing and flooding down my cheeks.

"I know," he mumbles back.

I look up at Puck as he walks into my cell and drops down on the shitty mattress, holding me in his arms.

"I know."

FOR MANY WEEKS, the only emotions I can fathom are grief and despair. I'm lost and angry and ready for revenge, but at a loss on what to do. Me and Puck have each other's back throughout. But even though I'm hurting and grieving the loss of my poor innocent sister, there's still one thing that won't leave my mind.

Theo.

And I hate that even after everything that's happened, I'm wasting my time thinking of her.

I never replied to her that day and I have no idea if she was waiting for me. But I do know this. As much as she made *me feel alive, I can't shake the feeling that if I wasn't so caught up in her, I might have noticed what was going on at home more. If I wasn't sneaking out or constantly talking to her, I might have noticed my sister was pregnant and in trouble.*

*What happened wasn't Theo's fault. But my actions were. And for that, I hate Theodora Harlow.*

I SIT AT MY DESK, nursing a bottle of Jack, trying to gather my thoughts. Thinking back to nine years ago brings up emotions I'd long since buried. I let my feelings towards Theo turn sour, using her as the thing to blame for all my problems back then, all because I was happy. How could I have been so happy when my sister was pregnant and struggling?

But thinking about it now, I know I was wrong. Theo wasn't to blame for my problems. If anything, she helped. Instead of completely drowning in grief, I had memories of her to keep me afloat. Whether they made me angry or not.

I grab my phone off the desk and scroll back to that one message I'd received just over two years ago.

**King, are you there? I need someone.**

The message from Theo still sits in my inbox unanswered.

When I got out of the prison after a year, I never reached out to her as much as I'd convinced myself I should have. Too much had happened and I couldn't handle my emotions.

Besides, it had been a year. I was sure she'd found someone else.

But two years ago when this text came through, I didn't know how to react. So I ignored her. Again.

It wasn't until a couple days later that I'd found out her mother had died. She was reaching out to someone and I wasn't there for her. So how could I reach out again?

I didn't know that Theo was holding onto that moment I abandoned her all those years ago, just like I didn't even realise I was holding onto the memory of her to keep me going for all these years.

I need to tell Theo why I left her nine years ago and why I've hated her ever since.

But I don't hate her.

Not even a little bit.

## 25.
## Theo

After yesterday's antics and my showdown with King, I snaked my way through the corridors and finally found the bedroom I'd been staying in and locked myself in.

I curled myself up in the sheets and cried. Cried for what my life had become.

I miss my mum. I miss Puck. I miss the King I used to know. I hate feeling so weak, but I need to let it out. I need to accept what my life is now.

This morning, I showered, smiling to myself, remembering how Puck would hide me in those awful communal showers. I decided to predict the weather. I closed my eyes and felt him barricading me in. I talked to him for what felt like hours before I opened my eyes and remembered he wasn't there and that he wasn't coming back.

The shower had gone cold, so I got dressed and went for a walk to clear my head.

The view from the Rhivers mansion is extraordinary. Woodlands on one side and an expansive lake on the other. I make a mental note to explore as much as I could before going back to the prison. I'd miss this for sure.

My stomach clenches for the millionth time this morning

and each day is getting harder to cope. The grief of losing Puck strikes me deeper every day. The weight of my relationship, whatever that is, with King is dragging me down. I feel like I'm caught up in a riptide. The harder I try to get out of it, the faster I drown.

"Excuse me," a small, timid voice calls from behind me and I turn to see a woman, smaller than me, holding a cup of tea. And I don't need anything else other than the bright brown eyes and warm smile to know that this is Puck's mother, Maria. And the riptide takes me under. The tears overflow and I fall against the low brick wall outlining the house.

"Oh, dear, please don't cry. You'll set me off," she speaks in a motherly tone, placing the tea on the wall next to me and sitting on my other side.

"I am so sorry," I sob as her hands find mine.

"Now, dear, I'll have none of that. This is not your fault, do you understand me?" she demands and I slow my sobs to low whimpers.

"I heard my boy was very fond of you," she says and a small, sad chuckle leaves my lips.

"I was just as fond of him, ma'am. I wouldn't be here without him."

She looks at me with a smile and I avoid her eyes, the pain slicing through my heart.

"He would've been here if it weren't for me, though."

Maria tuts at me and lifts my face to hers, holding me close with both hands.

"My boy had a heart of gold. He would've done it again and again if it meant helping those he loved. If he loved you that much, then I do too."

I sit in silence, trying to calm my tears and find the right words.

"Your silence is everything, my dear," she says and I smile.

"He didn't know if you were alive. It was hurting him so badly to not know if you were still alive." I hiccup as I watch a lone tear escape down her cheek.

"And he will know that I am, dear. I'm sure he's looking at us right now, telling us to stop being so dramatic."

I laugh a genuine laugh and look up into the sky again, thankful it's a sunny day. My favourite kind.

"That sounds like Puck."

After a couple moments of silence, she stands and nods to the tea, patting down the apron around her waist.

"Are you staying here?" I ask, wondering if she's still a maid for the family.

"As long as King will have me." She smiles, and I know King would never let a bad thing happen to this woman from what I know of his relationship with Puck.

"Good. Because I've heard you make the best mac and cheese."

She laughs and bends down to kiss my forehead before heading back inside and I take a moment to smile up at Puck, hoping he's found peace.

"Theodora," a soft voice calls out, echoing through the fresh air surrounding the garden.

I turn around to see Rori walking towards me, her silver

hair flowing around her shoulders effortlessly, a small braid neatly weaved into the curls. She really is flawless.

"Hi," I reply quietly, turning back to stare out at the view as she meets my side.

"Look, Theodora," Rori begins, but I interrupt her.

"It's Theo," I say with a small smile.

"Right," she says, shuffling on her feet.

I fold my arms across my chest and keep my head forward, waiting for what she's about to say.

"Look, I don't know you. Dax and King both have very different opinions about you."

I turn my head and cock an eyebrow and she laughs gently.

"Well, anyway, regardless of both of them, I make my own opinions on people. I don't know how I feel about you yet. You've caused problems in my home and I'm protective of my boys."

Her revelation takes me by surprise at how comfortable she is talking about the Rhivers mansion and *her boys*. A slight pang of jealousy worms its way through me.

"Your home?" I question. I tell myself I'm just curious and not nosey as fuck, but we both know the truth.

She smiles at me, which seems like a genuine smile.

"Yeah. My home," she confirms. "But what I will say is thank you for taking down that motherfucking son of a bitch." She laughs and I study her.

"Carlo?" I question, even though she can't be talking about anyone else.

"Yes. The bastard got what was coming to him."

I nod and look back out at the view. I don't know how to feel about Rori, but I'll take a friend if I can get one.

"We're not friends," she says and I panic, thinking I've just voiced my thoughts out loud. "Like I said, I don't know you and I'm protective of both Dax and King. They're my family and so far all you've done is cause trouble. But I respect you. I want to be upfront. I haven't got a problem with you, Theo," she says, then turns her whole body to face me. I look into her eyes as she finishes her speech. "But if you hurt either of them, I most definitely will hurt you."

I nod and accept what she's saying. I have no idea how long she's been here. I definitely don't remember King ever mentioning her before, but who am I to disagree. If it were me, I'd be the same. Of course she's protective of her family.

"I understand. However, I think it's impossible to hurt *him*." I emphasise, meaning King.

She peeks over my shoulder and smiles slightly before looking back at me.

"You'd be surprised." She winks and then walks off in the direction she came.

I turn to look back at the view when a presence on my other side startles me.

King stands quietly to my right, looking out at the view. Instead of his pristine suit, he's wearing suit trousers and a crisp white shirt, unbuttoned at the top. His sleeves are rolled up and his tattooed skin moves like a piece of art as he swipes a hand through his messy hair, his classic fedora nowhere in sight.

I check out my choice of outfit and cringe at my plain long-sleeved, white summer dress hiding my scars and sitting softly mid-thigh. My dark hair is swept up in a messy bun and my eyes are almost swollen shut from crying. But him. How can he make looking like shit look so good?

"You look like shit," I say, turning away from him.

A slight chuckle comes from him, which startles me. He seems so relaxed.

"Come with me?" he asks, stepping slightly ahead, down the bank towards the lake.

I look between his eyes and contemplate going with him. He does look like shit. Like he's been up all night. Maybe our brawl affected him a little more than I thought it ever could.

"Please, Theo." He sounds defeated, using my name instead of Theodora, which he likes to wind me up with.

I nod once and follow him slowly down the hill.

***

KING LEADS me down towards the lake and we follow it along in complete silence. The lake is starting to meet the trees and eventually, we're well within the depths of the woods, the lake still on our right side as we walk alongside it.

It's peaceful out here. The wind is gently blowing the leaves, rustling them against each other. The sky is a bright blue, sticks crunch under our shoes, birds tweet in the clouds up above, and the water calmly sails next to us.

The silence is deafening and I hate the uncertainty of it, but I also can't think of anything to say.

After fifteen more minutes of silent walking, the lake turns into a wider pathway and crashes of water disturb the silence. I look around, searching for the source of the noise, until we walk into a clearing and in front of us is a huge, beautiful waterfall, one that looks so much more breathtaking than I remember.

My heart cramps and my emotions flare as I take in the sight before me, old memories bubbling to the surface and threatening to combust. I look over at King, who is staring straight ahead, and I can only imagine he's thinking the same thing.

"I haven't come back here since," he says quietly but loud enough for me to hear over the spray.

"I didn't know it was so close to your house," I reply just as quietly. Quite frankly, I have no idea what to say. Why would he bring me back here?

"King, I can't." I take a step back.

Being here with him, it hurts.

"Theo," he says, turning back to me.

"No, King. No." I raise my voice. My eyes scan the waterfall as I recall that night nine years ago. "You said don't go anywhere. *You* said that!" I almost shout at him, remembering how he asked me to stay, but then he left me anyway.

"I know," he replies. "Please just hear me out."

"You're kidding, right? Nine years is now deemed enough time to clear the air, is it?"

"Nine years has been way too long. Theo, I didn't even know you still thought about us from back then. It's been so long."

"I tried, King," I shout, losing all patience. "I waited for you. All night. I woke up on the fucking ground outside the gates. You never showed. You never answered my text to say you were bailing. You never replied ever again."

"I know," he repeats again.

"My mum *died* and even after years of no contact, I bit the bullet, knowing you'd know out of anyone how it felt, and you still didn't reach out to me when I needed you!" My breathing gets faster as my anger boils. "I NEEDED YOU, KING!" I shout, left completely naked and vulnerable in front of him. I drop down onto the ground and hug my knees to my chest and bury myself, waiting for the ground to swallow me up.

My tears threaten to fall, but I keep them at bay. I've cried enough over him.

"Bonnie, my sister, died that night," he says after a couple minutes of silence. "That's why I never showed. My father had just shot her. Then threw me away for witnessing it."

I stay silent, not knowing how to respond. I look up at King, still facing the waterfall, but his face is scrunched up with pain, his eyes glassy.

"My sister Bonnie, she was hidden, she was—"

"I know," I say softly and he turns to look at me. "Puck."

I couldn't let him go through telling me. It looked too painful. He nodded and continued.

"I was with Puck when my father came in, beat him, and carried him away. I got knocked out and had no idea what was going on. When I came round, I was in my room, so I went to look for Bonnie and Puck. Instead, I found my father coming out of the cells, discovering what he'd just done." His voice cracks and my heart cracks along with it.

"King, you don't have to say any—"

"I do," he says and sits down next to me, keeping some distance. "I confronted him and said I'd make him pay. He threw me in prison, which turns out is where he'd put Puck. Puck said that Carlo had said it was punishment for getting Bonnie pregnant and he'd have to live with the fact she was dead and he was rotting in a cell."

I frown at King's confession, saddened that Puck went through that. Puck didn't give me the whole story and now I understand why.

"I was there until I *'accepted the way things were and was ready to go back and help my father run the District'*. I sulked for a long time. So did Puck. It wasn't until I received a letter from Dax, after around eight months of being in there, that I stopped sulking. I still have no idea how he got it there, but he filled me in on everything back home and that he'd learnt about the prison and would be ready and waiting for revenge when I got back." King sighs and I sit silently, waiting for the rest of the story. "Me and Puck got sick of doing nothing, so we came up with a plan. I decided to wait it out a bit before confessing to my father that he was right to do what he did. Some stupid way of proving my loyalty. Eventually, after a year, he let me out. Me and Dax were going to take Carlo down, then Puck would be free and we could all try to move on as a family. Of course that didn't happen. It was getting harder and harder for me and Dax to plot against Carlo. He was always watching his back against us."

I think over everything he's said and take it all in. It seems bizarre that they couldn't kill Carlo considering they all lived together, but with Carlo already suspicious of them because of everything, it makes sense. He wouldn't expect a hit from Theodora Harlow when he was watching his son so closely, his most likely assassinator.

"But that's why I left you, Theo. I didn't bail on you. I was forced away."

I recall that night I fell asleep on the ground just outside my home, crying myself to sleep that I could be so foolish waiting around for King when in fact he'd just been a witness to his sister's death and then thrown into prison.

God, this was fucked up.

"What about two years ago? You said you were locked up for a year?" It feels silly to be questioning him on this when there are much more important parts to his story, but he wanted a chance to explain why he hurt me.

"I was a dick, Theo." He sighs, wiping his hands down his face. "You know, aside from Bonnie, all I could think about was you. Our conversations, this goddamn waterfall, your blue eyes that I could easily drown in. I was so torn on how to feel. I loved having thoughts of you to escape to, but I was so angry that I was even thinking about you at all. What right did I have to be happy?"

I just nod along, not really knowing whether he wants me to reply or not.

"Theo, you were like a saving grace to me in there. I had Puck, but it was you who kept me human, keeping alive the moments of anger and hope. I kept thinking about how I'd find you when I got out. But then I did and I didn't know what to do. Me and Dax got so worked up trying to put plans together and it had been a year, I didn't even think you'd be thinking of me. So I just left it. Then I got your text when your mum died some years later. And I just panicked. I couldn't be there for you and I have no idea why." His words are all jumbled up as he tries to get them out. "Theo, I don't have a good excuse. All I know is you never deserved to be treated or ignored the way you did and for that I am sorry. But at the time I had to put my family first. Christ, I was seventeen. I didn't know what the fuck I was supposed to do. My father had just murdered my sister. My father had just thrown me into jail. I—"

"It's okay, King," I whisper.

"I never meant to abandon you."

I look at him and I can see the truth in his eyes and my heartstrings tug even harder.

"We were just kids," I say back.

King hurt me. A lot. But after hearing what he went through, I can't hold a grudge against the seventeen-year-old boy I knew. He wasn't him anymore.

King stands and holds his hand out to me. I consider him, then gently put my hand in his and let him help me up. He walks us slowly around the waterfall's edge, up onto the rocks, until we're standing where we jumped off all those years ago.

Never letting go of my hand, King walks us to the edge.

"Ready?" he questions, and it feels like that word has more than one meaning.

I nod and with a step over the edge, we both fall into the depths of the water. But unlike before, King never lets go.

Under the water, King's grip tightens, crushing my hand until we both slowly come up for air and he pulls me into him.

Brushing my wet hair from my face, he holds me close and kisses my forehead.

"I'm not going to ask you again," he says, cupping my face in both hands. "But I'm not going anywhere."

# 26.
# Theo

I throw my arms around King's neck and kiss him like there's no tomorrow. I'm not sure what this is between us. Back then, I didn't know what King was to me, but I knew I had feelings I'd never felt before. And if I'm being honest about my feelings, nothing's changed.

King has always been something to me. I just don't know how deep it runs.

King's arms snake around my waist and travel lower, grabbing my ass and hoisting me up. I wrap my legs tightly around his waist, his erection digging into my stomach.

My tongue slides straight over our lips and clashes with his. It's passionate and raw and vulnerable, just like my feelings.

I don't know if it's a result of everything that's built up between us these past few months, or being back here that's relit the fire, but I won't dare put it out.

King moves in the water, walking us towards the shallower end, never breaking apart from our kiss. My hands tighten in his hair, holding on so he never lets me go.

As we rise out of the water, King's shirt is flattened

against his chest, defining all of his muscles as he moves me effortlessly through the water.

Reaching the edge, King lifts me slightly and sits me down on the rocks, pulling away from me to look me up and down.

My white sundress is now see-through and my nipples are visible and poking out, an obvious giveaway to my state of desire. King's eyes linger on my nipples before tracing them all over my body.

Goosebumps coat my skin under his gaze and I bite my lip in nervousness. His eyes land there, a fire burning brightly behind them, and I let go of my lip. In an instant, King's teeth replace mine, biting down firmly before dragging my lip out and letting it go.

A gasp falls from my mouth and I rub across my lip as a reflex whilst the tingling continues after his bite. King leans in and runs his tongue across my lip, replacing the first sensation with another, and my eyes automatically close as a pleasurable sigh leaves my lips.

"Lie down, Theodora," King whispers against my lips, stern and completely in control, knowing I will do just as he asks. I smile and pull away, slowly lying down on the rock, my legs still in the cold water from the knees down.

King grabs both my wrists and leans into me as he pushes them above my head. Leaving them there, he moves back down and his hands land softly on my thighs, his fingers fiddling with the hem of my dress that's heavy from the water.

Agonisingly slow, he lifts my dress up over my thighs and stomach, and I raise my ass in the air so he can lift it higher up my body. King peels my dress teasingly over my skin until it rests just above my exposed breasts.

Holding tightly onto the dress, King leans down and swipes his tongue over my left nipple, swirling and sucking until I'm panting for more. Letting it go with a wet pop, he moves on to the other and teases the same.

Every sexual encounter I've had with King has been feral and hungry, but this is different. He's taking his time and savouring me instead.

King slowly moves lower, his hands following his mouth in a gentle caress until his face ends up directly between my parted legs. His hands curl around my underwear and in one firm grasp, he rips them from my body and throws them into the water, floating along without a care in the world, just like all my inhibitions.

Before I get any time to think about it, King's mouth is on me and my eyes roll back as he licks me up and down without pause. His tongue massages my clit with a desperate need, swirling in all different motions, fogging my thoughts.

I jerk my legs out of the water and hook them around King's neck as he buries himself further into me. I rock on his face, my moans echoing around the crashes of the water. I open my eyes to take in the moment and watch as King's face is buried in my pussy, devouring me like his last meal.

Around us, the waterfall falls peacefully, whites and blues shining in the sunlight. The trees stand tall, shadowing us from everything, their leaves swaying gently in the wind.

My body is glistening with water droplets and my skin is golden from the sun shining directly onto us.

King's shirt is more soaked through than before. His

hands are roaming all over my breasts and stomach, tweaking my nipples.

As I watch him eat me, I lose my inhibitions all over again and rock harder against him, getting more turned on by his enjoyment in being buried between my legs.

The pleasure builds and I moan deeply just as my orgasm crests, but King takes his hands away and grabs my ankles, dropping them back in the water and pulling away from me.

His face is glistening from my wetness and he licks his lips, looking right at me.

For a slight moment, I panic that he's once again rejecting me and denying me my orgasm. Another game of his to destroy me. But his hands then fumble with his trousers, and as he pushes them down his legs, I let out a breath of relief.

He pulls his cock out and fists it before lining himself up with my entrance.

In one swift motion, he slams straight into me, in and out, hard and fast.

The lover is gone and my fucker is back.

I scream as I feel him deep inside me, hitting every nerve ending as he pushes into me right to the base of his dick.

"King!" Black dots cloud my vision at the high he's giving me.

With every thrust, my body is dragged up and down the rock, grazing me, but I don't care.

King grunts, his fingers digging harshly into my hips as he watches his dick slide in and out of me.

"So fucking long I've thought about fucking you on these

rocks," he growls out. "So"—thrust—"fucking"—thrust—"long."

My legs flail wildly, splashing water with each pound from King's hips.

"Oh fuck," I shout, just about ready to come. King takes that as his cue and strums his fingers against my clit, and I let it go. "OH FUCK!" My orgasm takes over, my core pulsating on his dick.

"That's it, sweetheart, fucking finally!"

I continue to ride my orgasm and seconds later, King follows, a feral moan escaping his lips as he empties himself into me.

His pace never lets up until every last drop of King has sunk in my pussy and my own cum coats his dick.

We're both breathing heavily, and I'm unable to take my eyes off of him as he continues to stare at our connected bodies. Slowly, he pulls out of me and I look down at his dick that's shining with both of our releases.

King continues to stare at my open legs and licks his lips as he watches my pussy pulse and empty of our desire. I notice him harden again instantly, not that his erection had gone, anyway.

"Fuck, Theo, you're going to kill me," he says, shaking his head and dipping under the water to cool himself down.

I smirk, pleased he is just as affected by this thing between us as I am.

A FEW SECONDS LATER, King appears out of the water and pushes his hair back off his face. He looks over at me, takes in my smile and still open legs, and drags his hands down his face.

Walking over to the edge, he steps out of the water and pulls his sopping shirt over his head. His torso is dripping with water and glistening, defining his abs even more than usual.

He walks over to me like the god he is, his trousers still undone and open as his cock sits high and proud, prodding him in the stomach. I guess his little dive under the water didn't help cool him off.

He stands over me, leans down to kiss me, and stands back up tall, but before he can move away, I reach up and grab his hips. I dig my foot into the rock and push myself up slightly so my neck is resting just on the edge, my head unsupported as I hold it up.

Positioning myself just under his shaft, I wrap my arms tighter around his ass and lick his dick from the base to the tip and back again. King sucks in a sharp breath and his dick twitches at the contact.

"What are you doing, sweetheart?" he asks, a deadly glint in his eye.

I look up at him, then hang my head lower and suck his balls gently. My tongue swirls around them, my nails digging into his ass.

"Theodora," he warns. But whatever he's warning me about, I don't take it seriously. He can deny it all he wants, but I know he wants this.

I move away and extend my neck just a little more so my

head is resting against the side of the rock, my throat exposed, and I open my mouth wide, inviting him in.

King stares down at me, flicking his gaze from my eyes to my open mouth, and only when he can see I'm not letting up does he slide his dick slowly into my mouth.

Holding on to the rock with one hand and the back of my head for support with the other, King pushes himself in and out of my mouth, slowly and cautiously. I can tell he's holding back, trying to be gentle.

King is big and I've never had him in my mouth before, but now that he's there, I don't want to let him go. I hollow my cheeks and suck him hard as he pulls himself out and grunts loudly.

"Fuck it," he mumbles before slamming his cock straight back in, hitting the very back of my throat. My fingers dig harder into his ass and I gag on him each time he pushes forward.

King's moans get louder with each suck and my saliva dribbles out of the side of my mouth with every thrust.

The muscles in his ass tense and I'm sure he's going to have scratches from my clawing fingers.

"Open your legs wider," he commands, whilst he thrusts in and out of my mouth at a faster pace. I spread my legs, my knees bent whilst my feet balance me on the rock, so he has the best view of my pussy. I reach down and rub my fingers through my folds, soaking them with our cum from moments ago.

King grunts louder as I let him use my mouth and I pull my wet fingers away and raise them in the air for King to suck on. My fingers hit the base of King's throat as he sucks them dry and my nails dig deeper into his skin.

"Fuck, I'm gunna come, Theodora," he growls.

I've never liked him using my full name, but when he says it like this, I can't help but love it. Blood pools in my head, making me lightheaded from where I'm upside down and I moan over his dick, the hum sending vibrations straight to the tip of his cock, and he roars as his release spurts into my mouth.

Just as the first drop of cum squirts down my throat, King pulls out and releases the rest over my neck and chest.

I swallow down what I had in my mouth, tasting his warmth and saltiness before lifting my head with King's help, and watch his cum drip down my body.

"Now I think you're really trying to kill me," he says, his tone one of pure sex, admiring his claim all over me.

I jump up unsteadily and walk to the edge of the rock, glancing at him over my shoulder.

"Not yet," I tease with a wink and jump in before he can say any more.

## 27. King

"He's just pulling up outside," Dax announces as he struts through the office, doing up the button on his blazer. I let out a frustrated groan, not wanting to deal with the visit from Kennedy Harlow today.

It's been just over a week since me and Theo called a truce at the waterfall, and I've rarely let her out of my sight since. Partly because now that I've feasted on her pussy with my mouth and dick, I can't get enough. But not today.

There's no way I was letting her see her father. More importantly, there's no way I'm letting him catch wind of the fact she's here and not still at the prison. So I locked her in my room.

She was sleeping peacefully after I'd worn her out. Sure, I had motives behind the fucking today, not just purely for our pleasure, but I needed her relaxed and tired out enough for me to leave her there and lock her in.

She'll give me shit for it, but what's new with us?

No, I need Kennedy Harlow to still believe she's rotting away in that prison.

Me and Dax have been working tirelessly these past few

weeks, trying to figure out who had a hit on Theo, and in result of that, who murdered Puck.

Kennedy is the only suspect who makes any sense, so I need information. Not only that, but we still haven't figured out who was anonymously transferring all that money to him right before the hit went out.

Shit smells bad, and it smells exactly like Kennedy Harlow.

I sit up straight, knocking my ankles off the edge of the desk, and gulp down the last two fingers in my glass. Dax rounds the desk and stands next to me, arms folded, with his game face on.

I rise from my chair and stand with him. We're equals. This District is ours, not mine. And Kennedy will continue to falter when he realises we're both reigning this empire. They all will.

There's a knock at the door before it opens, one of the guards ushering in Kennedy and discreetly closing the door, then disappearing after it clicks shut.

"Ahh, boys." Kennedy raises his chin, flicking his eyes between me and Dax before finally settling on me. I ignore his patronising comment, knowing he's trying to get under my skin.

"Kennedy." I nod to the armchair, insisting he sits. He does so, and I round the desk, pouring him a glass as I go. Handing it over to him, he takes a hesitant sip before putting it down on the table next to him.

"Mr Harlow, thank you for coming today," Dax says, ever the polite one in conversation.

"Jesus Christ, kid, how many times do I have to tell you to call me Kennedy?"

Dax just nods gently, but I smirk at how easy it is to rile him up.

"What do you want, Rhivers? I've got shit to do," he huffs.

I quirk my brow at the use of our last name. Last names in my line of business are usually used for an enemy, and this is just another tally in his long list of reasons not to trust him.

"We wanted to thank you for your payment for Theodora's placement at the District Prison," Dax starts.

"Long overdue," I butt in before Dax continues as if I didn't speak.

"Now that we have the money, her place is set and she can continue to stay there."

Kennedy huffs and rolls his eyes.

"Look, I don't give a shit where she stays. She lost any loyalty from me when she murdered an ally. A colleague. A friend, might I add."

I scoff at his endearments for my father, knowing it's all bullshit anyway.

"I can't have my District being jeopardised by your threats, so I paid. I'm hoping to move on. She's of no use to me now," he finishes, picking up his tumbler.

"Is that why you had her murdered?" I question casually.

Kennedy stills, the brown liquid sloshing in the glass at the sudden stop in movement. His eyes are wide and confused.

"She's dead?" he almost whispers, his face paling.

Interesting reaction for someone who says they don't give a shit.

"Funnily enough no, your guy failed. Managed to kill someone else instead." I squirm inside at my insensitivity to Puck, but I can't show any vulnerabilities in front of him.

"My guy... What? I—What guy?" Kennedy stutters out, confusion etched all across his features. My eyes narrow as I study him, trying to gauge whether he really didn't send a hit out on Theo, or if he's just that good an actor.

"Mr Harlow." Dax rounds the desk, perching on the edge of it. Kennedy looks around at Dax, not even registering the use of his name. "Theodora was almost stabbed. Had another cellmate not pushed in front of her, she would've died. The hitman was another cellmate, but no one of importance," Dax continues to fill Kennedy in. "He's dead. But he had to have instruction to murder her from someone. Now forgive us, Mr Harlow, for pointing the finger, but who else knows she's there but you?"

Kennedy's mouth is open slightly, his eyes unable to focus on one thing. He's thinking deeply. About an excuse, a lie, a plan, I don't know, but one thing is for sure. Kennedy didn't know his daughter was being targeted in that prison.

"I have no idea. I don't even know who—Why would I want to kill her?" he asks me.

I stand directly in front of him, looking down at him in his chair.

"You've already answered that one, Harlow. 'I don't give a shit where she stays. She lost any loyalty from me. I'm hoping to move on. She's of no use to me now,'" I mock, repeating his words back to him.

Kennedy stands so he's eye to eye with me.

"That doesn't mean I want her dead," he spits.

"You know, for someone who claims to have washed his

hands of his daughter, you seem awfully concerned about her," Dax says calmly, speaking my exact thoughts.

"What use is she to anyone if she's dead? Of course I'm concerned," he almost shouts, his temper rising.

I look back at Dax, suspicion lacing my thoughts.

"Forgive me, Kennedy."

He stops pacing and looks at me.

"But what use is she to *anyone* under lock and key in *my* prison?" I ask slowly, an evil glimmer in my eye.

I think back to those paychecks coming through and the mysterious subject that referenced 'for her', and I clench my fists behind my back, trying to compose myself.

Kennedy just stares at me, lost for words, realising he may have made one huge mistake in letting those words slip free.

"Apart from me, of course," I add just to spite him. I'd never intentionally hurt Theo, but he doesn't need to know that. "Let me get one thing clear here. Theodora Harlow is mine. She's tucked safely away in that prison where no one else can get to her apart from *me*. Dead or alive, she's no concern of yours anymore. She's no concern for anyone else. Her body, her words, her cries, her pleads, her fucking soul is mine and mine alone, and the next person who tries to claim her as theirs will not only be buried six-foot deep but will swallow the dirt as they go."

Kennedy is frozen to the spot as he takes in my threat.

"Mark my words, Harlow," I continue. "Whatever plans you had for your daughter are done with because the day you put Theodora in my clutches was the day you fucked up."

Kennedy slowly unfreezes and nods slowly. I wasn't discreet in my threat. I've made it fairly obvious that I know he has something planned for Theo and maybe that I even know about his suspicious transactions, but I'll let him stew on that.

"Right, well," Kennedy says, clearing his throat and smoothing his hands down his suit.

The door to the office opens, one of my men standing quietly on the other side, and I know Dax must've called for them discreetly.

"Mr Harlow is leaving now," Dax says to the guard, who nods and holds his arm open for Kennedy to follow.

Kennedy looks over at both of us and without saying another word, he leaves, back to his hell hole, to conjure up a plan B, I imagine.

---

I STORM UP THE STAIRS, a desperate urge to check on Theo now that Kennedy has left. I'm struggling to control my rage and it only heightens when I round the top of the bannister and stop at the loud bangs from the other side of my bedroom door.

I knew she wouldn't take well to being locked in, but does she have to be such a child? I have visions of my room trashed, the gold furniture broken to pieces, clothes and bed sheets strewn across the floor.

She's relentless. The banging never ceases as she continues to slam her fists against the door. I stand on the other side, just listening to her huff and puff before having to face her wrath.

"Fuck this." I hear her mutter before the pounding stops.

Her footsteps stomp through the room and I get the key out, satisfied she's not in close distance to punch me in the face when I open the door.

Just as I'm putting the key into the lock, I hear a loud smash and force my way inside to find Theodora standing on the other side of the room, holding a lamp in one hand. My gaze snaps to the floor-to-ceiling balcony door that's now in shattered pieces all over my bedroom floor, an identical lamp to the one in her hand amongst the broken glass.

"Are you fucking kidding me?" I shout, trying to understand what possessed her to smash my whole goddamn glass door down.

Theo jumps and looks over at me. Surprise and panic shine across her features for a split second before her anger returns, and she throws the second lamp in my direction.

I dodge it and run to her, grabbing her arms in both hands and pushing her up against the wall. She's trying to kick out of my hold, but I'm too strong. My hand makes its familiar way up to her throat and squeezes just enough.

"Why the fuck did you just smash my goddamn fucking window, Theodora?"

"Why the fuck did you lock me in your room, King?" she fires back.

I'm so angry after my showdown with Kennedy and now this, that I squeeze around her neck just a little bit tighter.

"Why are you complaining? I thought you loved being my little prisoner?" I spit and all too fast her hand connects with my cheek in a stinging slap, and I let go of her, stepping back slightly.

"Fuck you," she hisses, hurt by my words.

"God, Theodora, you're such a child," I reply, turning to

look at the mess she's made, the glass littering the floor. I drop my head and look at Theo's bare feet and legs, a cut on her ankle bleeding slightly from where a piece of glass must have nicked her. How can she be so stupid?

I look up at Theo and see her eyes are glassed over, tears threateningly close to falling. I step back into her and cup her cheeks with my hands, catching the tears that escape.

"Your father was here. I can't have him knowing you aren't at the prison," I tell her, trying to make her understand.

"Why couldn't you have just told me that?" she pleads.

"Right, because you would have listened to me if I told you to stay put?" I offer sarcastically with a raised brow and she tries her hardest to hide her smile.

"I'm not a child," she huffs out, just like a child would do. It's cute.

"Hmm," I murmur and kiss her neck. "Regardless, you're paying for my fucking window."

She rolls her eyes as I get down on one knee in front of her and lift her foot to rest on my bent knee.

"But considering you have no money, we'll have to think of something else, hmm?" I whisper as I bend down and lick the small drop of blood dripping from her ankle.

Theo doesn't take her eyes off me as I continue to lick up her shin, over her thigh, and down to her core. I plant a gentle kiss over her pussy through her shorts, place her leg down, and stand.

Curling my hand back around her neck, I kiss her deeply, passionately, hating myself for missing her earlier and hating the thought that goes through my head when I think of what Kennedy may have had planned for her.

"Your body, your words, your cries, your pleads, your fucking soul is mine, sweetheart, and mine alone," I mumble against her lips, reminding her I own her just as I did her father. "Do you understand?"

She pulls back and smiles, bringing her hand up to tighten around mine that's holding her throat.

"You're my King." She winks and I can't help but smile at her play on words with my name.

"Hmm, that's right, Theodora. And I'll be damned if you're not my queen."

## 28. Theo

I clamp my thighs together, my pussy aching for the punishment King is promising me. I look down at King's white shirt that's covering my black lingerie and slowly start to unbutton it. King groans and steps closer, his hands coming up to the shirt impatiently.

"Uhh-uhh," I tut, shaking my head, stopping him from helping.

After batting his hands away for a second time, King lets out a growl and within seconds, he's whipped his hands behind his back and secured a cuff around my wrist, the smirk on his face smug as fuck.

"What the fuck!" I try to jerk, but the cuff is clasped tightly and King yanks me forward, pinning me to his body.

"You should know by now, Theodora, that I don't wait for anything, and I certainly won't wait to take you."

"Have me," I correct him, gritting my teeth as he pulls my other arm behind my back, securing it into the handcuffs.

"No, sweetheart. *Take you.* I told you you're mine, mind, body, and soul. If I want to have you, then I'll ask for your permission. But you're already mine, Theodora Harlow, so I'm taking what's mine."

King steps back and looks me up and down. Hands bound above my ass, my chest pushed forwards, and with calloused fingers, he pulls the top of the shirt away from my body and peers down the white material.

"Mmm, you really are a sight to behold, Theodora." With strong hands, he rips the shirt right open, baring my body for his eyes to feast upon.

My chest is partially covered in a black harness bra, my nipples covered in lace, but strips of material case my breasts in three different directions. My black lace thong matches, with three thin strings decorating my hips, exposing my skin. King's shirt hangs loosely off my arms, pooling at the wrists where I'm handcuffed behind my back.

Scooping me into his arms, King walks across the shards of glass covering his black carpet, his shoes crunching the glass into even smaller pieces.

Throwing me on the bed, I land on my side and look up at him, scowling, and in an awkward position, but King just smiles and starts to undress himself.

"On your knees, sweetheart," he says, helping me up into a kneeling position at the foot of the bed. Climbing in front of me, King lies effortlessly on his back, one hand tucked under his head to support it.

Without waiting for further instruction, I shuffle on my knees so I'm straddling his hips and resting my lace-covered pussy against his bare cock that's standing proudly.

"Seeing you handcuffed is almost as breathtaking as the first time," he groans as I start to rub up and down on his dick.

I think back to that night all those months ago, to King walking me through the prison building, guiding my cuffed hands forwards, his back pressed a little too close to mine for someone you consider an enemy.

"You weren't a very nice man then," I say and watch him cock a brow, his hands finding their place on my hips, guiding me up and down his length.

"I'm not a nice man now," he challenges back.

"You let your men see me naked. You let a lot of men see me naked," I whisper at him and his body stiffens, a strong hand gripping my throat in its usual place, dragging me forward so we're nose to nose.

"I'll shoot every motherfucker who saw you naked," he seethes.

"Good job Dax didn't look then, hmm?" I mock and his grip around my throat tightens.

"Uncuff me, King, let me play." I smile, a mischievous look in my eye that I know will bring him around.

King leans over to the bedside table and retrieves a key that he must've placed there earlier and, reaching his hands behind my back, unlocks one of the cuffs. I sit up and place my palm out in front of him, asking for the key.

King places it into my open hand and leans back, his head resting on his arms whilst he watches me unlock the other cuff to free my wrist, when a shit-eating grin plasters its way across my face.

"What are you smiling at, sweetheart?" King questions, and I lean down to kiss him passionately on the lips, distracting him whilst I fiddle with the handcuffs, looping them through the bars.

"Just how much I'm looking forward to seeing you cuffed up for a change." I pull away and before he can consider my words, I cuff both wrists to the gold metal frame and admire my handiwork.

Jerking his hands away, he realises he's fucked and watches me swirl the key around my finger.

"Oh, how the tables have turned." I smile and stand up on the bed, looming over him.

"Theodora, uncuff me right now," he spits as anger radiates from him.

"No, I think I'm going to have a little fun first. But don't worry," I reply, shrugging the shirt from my arms and onto the bed at my feet. "I'll make sure it's fun for you, too."

I kneel back down onto the bed in between his widened legs and lower my head to his erect cock that seems to be harder than it was before. Maybe King likes to be restricted and that's why he gets off on doing it to me.

"Theodora," King says, irritated but aroused.

I lick his shaft from the base all the way up to the tip, licking off the precum that's beading, and watch him shudder, his cock jerking in pleasure.

After teasing him a little more, I stand and hook my fingers under the thin strings that sit on my hips and pull them down, baring my pussy for him. Slipping one finger into my folds, I moan as I swipe my clit and pull it away to reveal it glistening in my wetness. I lean over and place my finger in King's mouth, his tongue swirling around it, and I let it fall out of his mouth with a small pop.

"Want more?" I question and lick my lips.

King doesn't react, just stares at me, fighting the battle of arguing with me over his cuffed wrists or just enjoying the moment. Without giving him any more time to respond, I step over his chest and lower myself to my knees so I'm hovering just over his face.

King inhales and my stomach clenches, butterflies swarming around, my cheeks blushing.

"Sit down, Theo," he murmurs and I do as he says, his mouth instantly latching onto my pussy, sucking and licking like a starving man.

A loud moan escapes me as he devours me and my hips rock back and forth on his face. King has feasted on my pussy many times, but this is unlike anything before.

My thighs clamp around his head as I rock my hips mercilessly, his mouth sucking on my clit, his tongue dipping into my entrance every few seconds. I rock my hips faster and faster, and the noises we make together urge me on.

King's hands clasp around the bars, his knuckles going white with the force, and I look down to see him completely buried beneath me and with one last flick of his tongue, I come apart. King never lets up and draws my orgasm out of me for what feels like minutes.

I slow my hips down and lift myself off King's face and hear him take in a deep breath, licking his lips clean. His face is glistening in my cum and he looks proud of it.

"Sweetheart, I could drown in your pussy every day."

I blush and shuffle down his body, impaling myself straight onto his dick in one solid thrust.

He moans. The most beautiful sound I've ever heard comes from his mouth and I swallow it down with a kiss, tasting my release on him and moaning back into him.

I lift my hips up and down slowly, and an impatient growl escapes King's lips.

"Theo, uncuff me. I need to touch you." I continue to grind up and down his shaft. "Now!"

I fumble for the key on the sheets and hastily uncuff King from the bed frame. As soon as he's released, he switches us round, my back on the bed, without breaking our connection, and replaces the cuffs onto my wrists once more.

"You ever cuff me again, Theodora," King threatens, his thrusts hard and fast as he pounds into me, "you'll be back in that cell downstairs and this time, I won't come and fuck you in it."

A scream rips from my throat as he twists me up onto my front, lifting my hips so I balance on my knees, my chest and face pushed into the bed.

King slaps a palm onto my ass and the bite of the sting makes me hiss. My arms cross awkwardly above my head and I turn to look at King, admiring his red handprint on my ass.

"Fuck, Theo," he rasps, a strong hand reaching down to grab my neck. His fingers squeeze, my pulse beating rapidly, in time to his thrusts.

"King, I'm gonna come," I whisper, barely able to get any sound out.

"Come for me, Theodora. You're mine, Theo, and I'm going to take everything from you. Every word, every tear, every last drop of cum. Come for me."

And I do.

A scream erupts from my throat, constricting against King's fingers, my body shaking with a tidal wave of pleasure as my orgasm takes over any coherent thoughts.

King follows after, draining himself into my pussy, not letting up until every last drop is gone.

We fill the silence with heavy panting and our skin glistens with sweat, my hair sticking to my neck. King slides out of me and admires my pussy for a couple minutes.

"I mean it, Theodora," King says, turning me back over. "Handcuff me again and there will be hell to pay."

"Nahh, I think you liked it." I laugh and wink at him, watching him shake his head and stand, leaving me cuffed to the bed.

"King!" I shout as he opens the door.

Turning back around, he throws me a wink before shutting the door behind him.

Asshole.

# 29.
# Theo

It's been a few weeks since I smashed King's balcony door and every day has been the same since. We wake up together, since I've unintentionally decided to sleep in his bed every night. We fuck, argue, and bicker about something completely juvenile like we're a couple of kids and it feels right. He then disappears into his office for hours to work, or whatever it is he gets up to, and I wonder about the house and the grounds. Rori has kept me company occasionally, but even after these past few weeks, she's still sceptical of me.

Today I'm bored, walking through the house, dragging my feet until I find myself back in the same corridor I was in when I first left the cell King had put me in. I walk slowly, eyeing up the portraits again and stopping at the last one that nagged at me previously.

The portrait of the District families looks back at me, all with happy smiling faces. My focus is on Carlo Rhivers and his smug smile. He appears invincible, sitting in his throne-like chair with the rest of the families crowded around him.

I wait for the guilt to wash over me, but it never does. I'm not sure how me of all people ended up being the one responsible for the death of Carlo Rhivers when you have the likes of King, easily skilled to do such a thing.

But I'm not one to trick fate. I know how lucky I was.

My gaze travels to Emily and her smile that doesn't seem to meet her eyes, her hand ever so gently resting on Carlo's shoulder. I wonder what kind of woman she was.

Without too much thought, I flicker over to Edison Ramon and his second, not paying much attention to the tall, dark-haired men before looking at my parents.

My father's arm is around my mother's waist in a protective grasp, but knowing a little more about my father now, I wonder if it was more possession than protection.

My mum's smile is soft and beautiful, just like her. How she came to marry a District Leader is beyond me. I wonder if she knew her worth. I wonder if she and Emily were friends like my father claimed to be with Carlo.

Leaving the portrait behind, I head towards King's office with a few of these questions on my mind. I've only been in King's office a handful of times, but considering it's where he spends most of his time, I know exactly how to find it in this mansion.

I hover outside the door and decide to walk in. We bickered this morning because I showered without him. I never denied our arguments weren't petty, and I thought to argue over something like that was beneath him. But I seem to have a way of getting under his skin, and I like to push his buttons.

Deciding I'm in the mood to irritate him further, I push open the heavy door without knocking. I know how rude it is, especially because he's working, and for one, if he ever did that to me, I would be fuming, but like I said, I want to get under his skin.

Without a care in the world, I stroll into the huge office and shut the door softly behind me, then turn to look at King.

He's sitting behind his desk, working on his laptop whilst his phone is lit up next to him with a male's voice coming through. It's obvious he's on a call and the death glare he's giving me is enough evidence to know he's still pissed at me.

I give him a soft smile and sit down in the large leather armchair opposite his desk.

King replies to whoever is speaking but doesn't take his eyes off me. I scan the space, taking in the floor-to-ceiling bookshelves, with books I know must've been Carlo's because King doesn't read, on both walls to my left and right and the floor-to-ceiling windows behind him overlooking the woods. It's beautiful.

Especially with the scowling man sitting in front of them.

I listen for a while, getting bored of the conversation that has absolutely no relevance to me, and King's eyes shine with humour when he realises my plan to bother him is only boring me.

I scan him up and down, taking in his shirt sleeves that are rolled up to his elbows, his inked arms a stunning piece of art on display. His few top buttons are undone, revealing more tattooed skin, and as my core clenches at the mere sight of his bare skin, a wicked idea comes to mind.

I stand up slowly, biting my bottom lip gently, and start to push the straps of my pink summer dress down my shoulders and arms. The scars are the faintest I've ever seen them, but since being with King, I'm not frightened of losing the

## ELLIE KENT

memory of my mother once they fade. Nine years away from King is enough proof that memories will stay with you for a lifetime. And he was right, all those months ago, back in the shower at the prison when he'd asked me about them. The scars on my heart are what I'll have left. I know that now.

King immediately realises what I'm doing and his scowl returns as he replies to whoever is on the phone.

I smirk as the dress slips down my body and pools in a heap at my feet. My naked body underneath catches King's attention and he groans so softly, wiping a hand down his face. Walking over to him, I gently reach across the desk, my breasts taunting him as they brush across his bare arm, my nipples standing to attention.

I reach for his fedora that I love on him so much and stand up straight again, putting it on my head, then walk back to the armchair. King raises his eyebrows at me, watching my every move, his eyes roaming over every bit of my body he can see.

I sit down on the armchair and swing one leg over the armrest so I'm wide-open and bare for King to see everything. His eyes are wide and the guy on the phone calls out his name before King clears his throat and responds.

I suck on my fingers, then trail my hand down my body in slow, teasing strokes, rubbing my fingers over my pebbled nipples. I take a handful of my breast and tug on my nipple hard, a small gasp leaving my lips, extended for King's benefit.

My hand travels south and I rub slow circles on my inner thighs, teasing him further, but the torture on myself is too much and the way he's staring at me with hunger only spurs me on.

I swipe a finger through my folds and moan softly, my eyelids fluttering closed for a few seconds. Opening my eyes, I notice King trying to readjust himself in his trousers and a thrill shoots through me.

I take my hand away and lift his hat off my head and place it directly between my thighs, hiding my pussy from his eyes, and my hand disappears behind the hat to play with myself.

I rub slow circles across my clit, my legs jerk involuntarily every now and then, and my moans come out breathlessly. King's gaze is blazing hot and if he wasn't so turned on, I know he'd be cursing me out for taking away his show.

I push a finger deep into my soaking core and let out a small whimper at the intrusion, revelling in the feeling, but also hating that I don't hit the spot like King does.

As I keep pleasuring myself behind King's hat, denying him from watching, I only turn myself on more. King goes to stand up, but I shake my head, warning him not to.

Surprisingly, he sits back down, anger flickering in his eyes before they turn to mischief, and his hands start playing with his belt. As he undoes it, he replies to whoever's on the phone, without a tremor in his voice, and then takes his hard dick out of his pants, grasping it in his hand.

I stall, my fingers stopping as I watch King stroke his shaft and rub his thumb over his tip, spreading his pre-cum. But before I can enjoy any more, King tucks himself under the desk and all I can see is the movement of his arm.

I pout, disappointed that I can no longer see what he's doing, until I realise he's giving me a taste of my own medicine. The hat still sits between my legs as I rub myself slowly and I know he's playing me at my own game.

Theo – 0 King – 1

No longer caring about my game, I put the hat back on my head and push two fingers into my core, clenching around them, using my free hand to rub against my clit.

King's eyes sparkle, knowing he's won, but he pushes his chair back and starts to tug on himself in my view again. I moan at the sight and work my fingers faster, but King pauses and puts a finger to his lips to shush me.

Crooking his finger, I follow it like a demand, tiptoeing softly on the hardwood floor so as not to make a sound.

"And what am I supposed to do with that information, Jones? It sounds like you're just leading me to a dead end," King says, replying to this Jones on the phone.

When I reach him, King positions me in front of him and bends me over at the hips, placing my hands on the edge of his desk. My cheeks heat up as I hear Jones's voice talk through the phone, which is suddenly very close to my head.

King lines himself up with my entrance and in one quick thrust, forces his way into me, hitting me deep, and a whine escapes my lips when he instantly hits that spot.

"What was that?" Jones asks at the interruption and I bite down hard on my lip, cringing that he heard me.

"Nothing, Jones, continue. I'm getting bored," King replies casually.

I turn around to look at him over my shoulder and he winks at me, bringing his finger back to his lips again. Grabbing a handful of my breasts in both hands, he gently moves me backwards so I'm sitting up on his lap, my back pressed fully against his chest, his shirt an irritating barrier between us.

As I'm flat against King, I can't help but moan again as his dick hits a whole new angle, pushing in deeper.

"Make another sound, sweetheart, and I'll turn this call straight to video so he can see you're just as much a dirty girl as you sound," King whispers in my ear and I turn to call his bluff.

King reaches for the phone and he holds it out in front of me, his finger hovering over the camera button. I know there's no way he'll do it, but the threat is enough to make me nod.

"Hold the phone, sweetheart," he whispers, pushing the phone into my hand.

My eyes widen as I try to protest, but he just thrusts his hips, and I bite hard into my lip as I try not to scream.

With the phone now in my hand, King holds both my hips to control my movements and he moves in and out of me in slow, torturous thrusts. My hand clenches around King's phone whilst Jones continues to babble away and my lip starts to bleed as I bite into it harder with each thrust to not make a sound.

"I will get the guys on it and pick up the pace," Jones says through the receiver and King chuckles quietly behind me and starts to thrust harder into my core, picking up his own pace as he slams his dick far deeper than he's ever been before.

I'm whimpering when all I want to do is scream and it's getting harder and harder to stay quiet. King thrusts and thrusts, one hand now clamped around my mouth. I bite into his palm, the other firmly on my hip as he moves me over his cock.

Just as I'm about to lose it, King takes the phone from my

hand and I don't care if he turns it into a video call. I just need to come.

"Good, get it done," King rasps and presses the end call button.

Throwing his phone down onto his desk, his hand comes away from my mouth and presses onto my clit.

"Fuck, Theodora," he shouts as I scream my release.

He drags out my orgasm, pounding into me, his thumb rubbing hard circles on my clit, extending my ecstasy. His cum shoots out of him seconds later, filling me up as my screams continue.

As our orgasms come to an end, our breathing falls heavy and my throat feels hoarse from screaming so loud. I turn my head and kiss King with the last of my energy, when the large office door crashes open and Dax and Rori both rush through, guns out in front of them.

"Oh my fucking God," I shout, trying to jump off King's body, but his dick is still so deep inside me I can't get off quick enough. My hands cover my breasts, my whole body blushing the deepest shade of pink, and King takes the hat from my head and drops it to my pussy, hiding what they've clearly already seen. King balls deep inside me with our cum probably dripping all over the place.

Dax looks mortified and mildly angry as he turns back around and grabs Rori by the wrist. Storming out of the room, Dax shouts over his shoulder, "We're going to need some boundaries, King. Fuck your girl in your own space so I don't think she's getting murdered."

Rori looks back over her shoulder, smiling at the sight, and as she's being dragged away, I hear her complain.

"Why have you never fucked me in the office?"

"Rori, shut the fucking door," Dax shouts, halfway down the hall, when Rori stumbles back and pretends to cover her eyes.

"Sorry," she squeaks out in a girly voice before slamming the door shut behind her.

# 30.
# Theo

The soft knock at the door is enough for me to know it wasn't King, so I call out a hello and sit up in the bed, my legs all twisted up in the covers.

"Uhh, hi," Rori's soft voice calls out as she pokes her head through the gap in the door.

"Hey." I smile, my cheeks already blushing again at the position she found us in hours ago.

Without another thought, Rori steps in and closes the door, then comes and sits next to me on the bed, her shoulders resting against the gold headboard. She looks over at me, so I lean back down again.

"Look, Rori—" I start before she interrupts me.

"I am not even sorry that we walked in on you." She starts laughing. "Damn, Theo, that screeeam!" She laughs some more.

I figure she's laughing at the situation and not at me, and a small chuckle escapes my lips. If I don't laugh, I'll cry, right?

"Fuck off, Rori," I say softly through my laughter, not really sure if we're at this level of banter.

She continues to chuckle a little more, then grabs the duvet and tucks herself underneath the covers.

"I've got to hand it to you. I think you'll give me and Dax a run for our money."

I roll my eyes at her.

"You and Dax are in love. That in itself is already giving *us* a run for our money!"

"Pfft, if you can't see King's in love with you, then you've got no hope," she scoffs.

"King is not *in* love with me, Rori. I'm just here at the moment," I reply.

"Oh, don't give me any of that attention seeking crap, Theo, you're better than that." She smiles wickedly and honestly, I feel a little caught out. "King hasn't had a girl here for as long as I've been here. You're definitely something to him."

"How long have you been here?" I ask, curious.

She looks up at the ceiling, nodding as if she's counting, then smiles.

"Seven years, give or take a couple months."

Wow, seven years is a lot longer than I thought it would be. I count down the years in my head and realise she would have been around seventeen or eighteen.

"King was in prison when Dax brought me here," she says softly, her eyes clouded over like she's deep in thought. I stay silent, waiting to see if she continues. "When King was away, Dax was all by himself. Got into some bad shit. Found me."

She looks at me again with a sad smile.

"But that is a story for another day… Let's go back to

talking about how good a fuck King Rhivers is. Maybe I ended up with the wrong cousin." She winks and I hit her arm, nudging her slightly. If I didn't already know how in love with Dax she is, I definitely wouldn't have let that slide.

She continues to laugh and the rest of the afternoon passes with just me and Rori, chilling in King's bed, eating snacks and watching trash TV.

I could be mistaken, but I feel like Rori is my friend and for that I'm grateful.

"Is EDISON RAMON GAY?" I ask innocently out of the blue and three sets of eyes all turn to me, confused.

We're sitting in the dining room, me, King, Dax, and Rori, eating our dinner after a lazy Sunday afternoon, when the portrait comes back to mind, the handful of questions I was going to ask King yesterday only just remembered.

"Umm, no. Why would you ask that?" Dax replies, cocking an eyebrow at my random question.

"Well, I was looking at the portrait on that corridor by the cells. There's a picture of my parents, Carlo and Emily, and Edison and some man. I didn't know if they were together or something?" I asked.

King chuckles slightly before answering my question.

"That's Casper Ramon. They're cousins and much like me and Dax, he's like Edison's partner, if you will."

I nod slowly, starting to understand.

"But why was he in the picture? What about his wife?"

"Edison never married. I guess Casper was in the photo because he helps run the Third District, like our mothers did alongside Carlo and Kennedy," King replies.

"He's fucking weird," Rori pipes up and I furrow my brows in confusion.

"Casper," she clarifies. "I've only met him a couple of times, but the dude doesn't speak. He just follows Edison around like a lost puppy."

"Yeah, he's quiet, but at least he stays out of drama. And the Third District seems to be the only one without it, running smoothly. Edison and Casper have never been a problem," Dax finishes.

"I have an idea," Rori says, cutting the silence. "Well, considering Carlo is now dead and no offence, but Elisa and Emily are, too, we should take a new picture. We could have one of the four of us and—"

"No." King's cold voice echoes through the room, stopping Rori from continuing.

"What do you mean *no*? The leaders have changed." Rori shrugs, ignoring King's tone.

"Yes, they have, Rori, but that doesn't mean we'd need the four of us," he says back with a blank facial expression.

A twinge of hurt travels through my gut as I take in his words but try not to take them personally.

"Theodora is a Harlow," he adds as if that's all the explanation needed.

*Ouch, that stings.*

I wince at King's statement but don't have it in me to reply. He's right after all. No matter how much it hurts to hear him talk about me like that. How can I stand next to his side when I'm the one responsible for killing his father and I should technically be the heir to the Second District?

"Then fucking give her your name and she won't be," Rori fires back, shrugging her shoulders, not backing down against King.

King lets out a hollow laugh, then fires back, "Don't be ridiculous, Aurora."

"It's not a bad idea," Dax chimes in and I roll my eyes at the three of them having a conversation about me as if I'm not here.

But we're talking about me marrying King here. Do I want that? Can we do that? It all seems to be moving too fast. Until King shuts it down.

"I'm not fucking marrying her," he spits and storms out of the dining room, leaving us all speechless.

Dax gives me a sympathetic smile and Rori just looks livid. But me? Without even realising what I want, the venom in King's statement crushes every bone in my body. How can Rori claim he's in love with me when the very idea of marrying me disgusts him?

I retire to my room for the rest of the evening and King never comes for me. I haven't slept in here since that first week and I feel very lonely in the large bed.

I thought me and King were past our hatred and denial. That afternoon at the waterfall was the line drawn. All cards were on the table and we said fuck it to all the bad blood between us.

So why does it now feel like it's coming back in bucketfuls?

A couple more days pass and King avoids me like a disease. He doesn't look at me or speak to me. If I'm sitting with Dax and Rori, he leaves the room, and I don't know what I did to deserve this treatment, but I'm over it.

King Rhivers has always been a master at manipulation and I'm just a naive little girl for falling into his trap more than once.

But no more. Send me back to that god-forsaken prison. Hell, send me back to my father for all I care, but I will not stand to be under his roof like this any longer.

I make my way through the ridiculously big mansion and find myself ready to burst into King's office, when I hear his raised voice coming from the other side of the door.

"I swear to fucking God, Harlow," he shouts and I flinch slightly, wondering if for a second he knows I'm here, but he shouts again. "Where did the fucking money come from?"

He must be on the phone to my father and I hesitate, deciding on whether to eavesdrop on King's side of the phone call.

My mother's warning suddenly rings through my ears and it's deafening.

"Never eavesdrop on a conversation not meant for you to hear, my darling. There will always be consequences."

But even with her words floating around my head, I can't pull myself away from the door, consequences be damned.

After a short silence, King speaks again, no longer shouting but spitting out his words with pure hatred.

"I told you, Harlow, she's mine. I don't give a fuck what you or anyone says. I will do what I please with her."

An involuntary shiver runs through my spine. He's said this before, but it was full of lust and admiration. Now it's full of possession.

"The next time you send another hitman to murder her, I will murder you, do you understand? Theodora Harlow will die at my hands when I'm done with her, not yours or anyone you pay. My hands."

I jump as a bang sounds from the other side of the door and a loud *fuck* is shouted through the air.

Shock paralyses me to the spot as his words play over in my head.

*"Theodora Harlow will die at my hands when I'm done with her."*

Is this why he's been avoiding me the past couple of days? Is this why he brought me here in the first place? Fucked with my feelings to make it easier for him to murder me?

He also insinuated that the cellmate who tried to kill me was instigated by my father.

Oh fuck. I can't breathe.

Dax walks out into the hallway and halts, his eyebrows drawn in worry as he looks at me.

"Theo, what's wrong?"

My eyes find his and they widen. Does Dax know? Is he in on it too?

I stumble backwards a few steps, mumble out a quick, "Nothing," and run. I don't stop until I reach my room and lock myself in.

The past few weeks come crashing down over me in a

dark cloud. He's used me and made me fall for him before he fucking kills me.

After all, I killed his father. Why would little Theodora Harlow be anything to him?

I need to get out of here.

Now.

# 31.
# Theo

I open the door quietly, hoping not to wake anyone. It's two in the morning and I've stayed in my room ever since I eavesdropped on King's phone call with my father. No one came to find me and that only made me more suspicious.

Dax saw me standing outside the door. He would've gone in and told King I'd heard whatever had been said. King knows that I know. God, what is this game he's playing?

My stomach growls again, reminding me why I'm trying to creep out of my room and down the hall. Walking with light steps on the soft carpet, I make my way silently down to the kitchen. Thankfully, it's empty and I haven't come across any staff yet.

Opening the fridge, I help myself to some leftover meat to fill the hole in my stomach. Only eating is making me nauseous, the uneasy feeling in my stomach never settling.

I take in my surroundings and figure out how I'm supposed to leave this place without being caught. I know there will be guards outside patrolling the area, but I have no idea how many or how often they circle. Maybe tomorrow I'll spend the day outside and see if I can spot a pattern.

A light switches on in the study just down the hall and I freeze, knowing it can only be King or Dax. I quickly shove the plate back into the fridge and walk to the other side of the kitchen to make my exit.

My eyes flicker to the kitchen knives stored on their magnetic strip, gleaming in the moonlight, and without a second thought, I grab one and run silently back to my room.

Once safe inside, I flip the lock and run over to my bed, kneeling at the side of the mattress. I slide the knife underneath, blade first, so I know I have a weapon of some sort if I need one.

I tuck my knees into my chest, my back pushed up against the headboard, and I take in deep breaths to calm my beating heart. My palms are clammy as I rub at my arms to stop the chill.

I have no idea what game King is playing, but he's winning and if I don't act soon, the game will be over.

I've been walked over all my life and I refuse to be trod on now. King Rhivers may be in the lead, but it's only a matter of time before he stumbles across a snake and slides right back down. And best believe that snake will be *me*.

THE NEXT DAY, I spend it doing just as I said I would, walking around the grounds and trying to suss out the guards' rota. There is a small change every two hours, but they just rotate, so there's never really any gap. So if I'm getting out of here, it's going to be pure luck because there's no way I can outrun the guards or go undetected.

The sun has long gone down and I've dressed in all black, to try and help blend into the shadows at any opportunity. My pulse hasn't settled for hours and the more I think about running, the crazier it seems.

I hadn't seen anyone at all today and it seems even more odd than before. Not even Rori has been around the grounds or to see me. Dax is avoiding me, or so it feels. A few times today I've caught the back of him as I turned to walk into another part of the garden. King is completely missing in action—I haven't seen or heard from him in two days now.

Something bad is going down and I need to be out of here before it does.

A loud knock comes at my door and I jump back a mile. Who the fuck is here now of all times?

The knock sounds again and that deep, husky voice I know so well calls out my full name.

"Theodora," King says, completely monotone.

I take a deep breath and walk towards the door.

"What do you want?" I reply quietly because if I spoke any louder, he'd hear the shake in my voice.

"I need to see you, Theo. It's been two days. My bed's cold without you."

I frown at the door, trying to figure out his angle. He sounds normal, but how could he be when we haven't even seen each other in two days? If normal is how he wants to play it, then so be it.

Shaking the tension out of my shoulders, I open the door to see King standing tall in his usual suit, minus the blazer. His white shirt is stretched across his taut muscles, the sleeves rolled up to show off his tattoos like usual.

"Look at me," he whispers and my eyes slowly travel over

his chest, his lips, until I finally land them on his. He looks sad, but I can't read him completely. Suddenly, sadness washes over me as I look into those green orbs.

His hand comes up to sit gently against my throat, in its usual spot, and his thumb rubs softly back and forth over my pulse point.

"Where have you been?" he asks, his eyes flickering between both of mine, trying to read me.

"Here," I reply and shrug, lifting my arm to gesture into my room.

"Theo, why are you avoiding me?"

"I'm not," I reply fast and he doesn't miss it, so I add, "You're avoiding me."

He lets out a little chuckle and bends low to kiss me softly on the lips before pulling me in close, his body flush against mine and his arms strong around me.

My arms find his waist and circle back around him, and we stand like that for minutes, letting the silence wash over us.

But my head is loud and clear. I can't let King consume me any longer.

"What are you thinking about so loudly?" King breaks the silence after a beat. I tense in his arms and he pulls back slightly to look down at me. His eyes scan my face, lingering on my lips, and under the pressure, I lick my bottom lip.

King takes that as his invitation and presses his lips firmly against mine, then pushes me back into the room, closing the door behind him with his foot.

And even though I know I shouldn't, I kiss him back and let him lead me to the bed.

My legs hit the edge of the mattress and I fall onto it,

King crawling above me moments later, our lips never breaking contact.

"You're a bit overdressed for this time of night, aren't you?" King jokes, bringing his lips back to mine, his hand rubbing up and down my jean-clad legs, and my whole world comes back to reality and what I was planning to do.

After King claimed my murder on the phone with my father, I haven't seen him once. I haven't seen anyone. King knows I know. Dax would've told him. So why the act? To lure me back into this false pretence that he does in fact love me?

My heart rate quickens again and panic floods through my veins.

I reach my hand down the side of the bed and stretch my fingers as I fumble for the handle of the knife I've hidden under the mattress. Our lips are rough and passionate as we battle it out with our tongues, fighting for love and for revenge. A goodbye.

Finally, my fingers feel the cold of the handle and I wrap my hand around it firmly and pull it swiftly out from under the mattress. Pulling my head back from King, I disconnect our lips and in one swing, lift my arm to put the blade under King's neck, the point already digging into his throat.

In one clean move, at exactly the same time I draw my knife, King's arm swings around his back and within seconds his gun is pressed harshly into the side of my head.

His expression is emotionless aside from his eyebrows that are drawn together slightly. I try not to show any emotion myself even though the barrel of his gun to my temple terrifies me. But I knew it was coming to this.

We're silent for many seconds, King hovering over me,

my knife held against his throat and his gun pressed firmly to my temple, our lips swollen and red.

He swallows, his Adam's apple bobbing against the edge of my knife before he speaks.

"What the fuck do you think you're doing, Theodora?" he questions, moving his head back slightly. But my hand follows and the knife never leaves his neck. King cocks his head at my actions.

His thumb flicks off the safety on his gun in retaliation and my eyes flicker to the gun at my head.

"Dax told me you were outside. You heard me talking to your father?" he questions, but it's more of a statement.

I keep still, my eyes latched onto his, my lips sealed shut.

Realising I'm not going to answer, King leans forward, his neck pressing against the sharp blade. Drops of blood slip down the knife and onto my hand, then drip onto my own neck as he hovers over me.

"You won't kill me," I whisper, not even believing myself.

A drop of blood lands right on my bottom lip and cascades down my chin, and King's eyes lock onto it, watching it descend down my throat. His eyes light up and he leans in even closer, the knife still digging into his neck.

"Won't I?" he challenges, then dips his head and trails his hot, wet tongue over the drip of blood, starting at the base of my throat and up to my lower lip. My pussy throbs as he licks and I curse my body for betraying me. Still, I keep my expression impassive.

"Or will you kill me first?" He smiles.

My hand tightens around the handle of the knife, my knuckles going white with the pressure. King pulls the gun away from my temple but slowly glides it down my cheek and over to my mouth, rubbing it across my lower lip, tracing where his tongue had been.

My chest heaves up and down heavily, my breathing frantic as he pushes the barrel of the gun between my parted lips.

"And I thought nothing would look more satisfying than my cock in this mouth," King taunts.

In slow movements, I release my solid grip around the handle and lower the knife away from his neck and to my side, waving my white flag in surrender.

King leans back and I take in the small little beads of blood glistening on his neck.

Looking down at my hand, the knife loosely in my grip by my thigh, then back into my eyes, he slowly pulls the gun out and I relax my mouth, the taste of metal strong on my taste buds.

"My stubborn girl has given in." He smiles.

"Never," I whisper, and before I can reconsider, I lift the knife and plunge it into his side, taking advantage of his shock to push him off me and crawl from underneath him.

A shot rings out. King growls and collapses onto his side, and I take my chance and run.

"THEO!" King shouts, the sound following me through the hallways as my bare feet run through the mansion.

Barely a minute later, King is on my tail, and as I haul open the large mansion door, I spin to look at him running across the landing towards me. The knife is gone, but his shirt is red from his bleeding wound.

I know I haven't stabbed him deep enough to kill, maybe only enough to leave a small scar, but King is running full force, knife wound or not, and bleeding out isn't going to stop him.

As fast as I can over the gravelled ground, I run. My feet cut and blister against the small pebbles, but I refuse to let it slow me down. I hear King behind me as another set of heavy footprints crunch on the gravel.

"Theodora!" King continues to shout. But I keep running.

I don't look back. I don't look around to see if any guards are on my tail. I run and I run until I reach the gates and pass through them.

Running out onto the road to disappear behind the trees, I have one last memory.

I hear King shout my name in panic. I see the blinding lights of the car coming straight for me and I feel the pain as my body is thrown over the car in force.

I ran from my protector and predator, only to be taken out by something entirely different.

# 32. King

I feel the ropes around my wrist and ankles before I open my eyes and shift uncomfortably on the chair. My ears are ringing and the pulse behind my swollen eye is echoing in my head.

Opening my eyes, my right eye only opening halfway due to the shiner I most likely have, I squint into the semi-dark room and try to gain my bearings. Looking down, I notice I'm tied to a metal chair, my shirt dark red from where Theo stabbed me.

Jolting my head up, I look around and opposite me sits Theo, tied to an identical metal chair. Her hair is scattered everywhere. There are red and black bruises covering her face and arms, and she's slouched, her head hanging off the back of the chair.

Anger courses through my veins as I process what's happened. Theo holding a knife to my neck, and in turn, my gun to her head. I would have never pulled the trigger, but I knew she was up to something and when I saw her hand reaching around the mattress, I knew she'd hidden something there.

I look back down to my side and remember the knife

cutting into my stomach. She hadn't even pushed hard enough for it to impale me, just cut deep enough for it to bleed.

With the adrenaline coursing through me, I chased her through the house and down the long driveway. I look at Theo's feet and see them all cut up, with dried blood coating her skin from where she ran across the gravel.

Then seeing the bright lights of the car and hearing the roar of the engine, watching Theo's body fly high over the car at the impact. She looked like a ragdoll, thrown into the air to crash back down onto the solid pavement.

I ran to her side, checked that she was still breathing, then turned back to the car that had stopped ahead, ready to give them a piece of my mind and use that gun Theo had held between her sweet lips not minutes before. God, that shouldn't turn me on half as much as it does.

Only when I looked up, a large boot smashed right into my stomach, knocking me down, then fist after fist came at me. I couldn't see my attacker as they had a black ski mask on. *Pussy.* Can't even beat me up and show their face.

Then I was knocked out and I woke up here, tied to a motherfucking chair in a dark room with a battered, bruised, and bleeding Theodora Harlow.

For what feels like hours, I continue to pull at the rope, try to wake up Theo and figure out where the fuck I could be and why, when finally, Theo starts to breathe heavier.

I look at her and see her chest rise and fall in fast heaves.

"Theo, you're okay," I speak quietly, letting her know she isn't alone.

I hear her small whimpers as she lifts her head up slowly and her chin hits her chest as she moves her head from side to side, trying to alleviate the ache in her neck from where her head has been hanging at an awkward angle for hours. Her hair is hiding her face, but I can hear her panicked breaths.

"King?" she questions, so quietly that if the room wasn't already deadly silent, I would've missed it.

"Yeah, Theo, it's me," I confirm.

Theo slowly lifts her head and shakes her hair away from her face, wincing, and her eyes latch onto mine. Her beautiful blues are full of pain and sadness, and cuts cover her usually flawless skin.

There's blood dried at her nostrils and the corners of her mouth, and deep purple bruises shade her cheeks.

She goes to sit up straighter, but her face scrunches up in pain and she stops moving suddenly.

"You've probably cracked your ribs, maybe broken a bone. You got hit by a car."

"I know," she replies, sarcasm and sass lacing her tone.

Even in the awful circumstance, a small smile escapes me at her attitude.

"Why the fuck are you still here pretending anyway?" she spits when she notices me smiling.

I cock a brow at her, any traces of my smile gone.

"Theodora, you may think I want to kill you, but I don't. And if you're insinuating I had anything to do with that car crashing into you, then you're way off. I have no idea who hit you, I have no idea who beat me up after running to your side, and I have no idea who the fuck tied us to these fucking chairs." I end up shouting, the anger coming back full force at her accusation and that she still believes I'm trying to kill her.

"Ahh, you're both awake," a male voice calls through the room. "Finally."

A tall figure appears from the shadows and a bang rings out as the door he just came through closes behind him.

"Miss Harlow, you were taking forever to come around," the voice says again, laced with amusement, and I try to recognise it, only nothing comes to mind.

Within seconds, the face of Casper Ramon comes into view right in the middle of us and I furrow my brows at him.

"King, good to see you." He nods at me.

I think of the handful of times I've met Casper Ramon. Edison Ramon's cousin, his second, helps the running of the Third District but never engages in conversation save for a few words. His portrait sits in my family home alongside my parents and Theo's, but he's never been anyone I've done business with unless he's with Edison.

I think back to his visit to my home a few months back when my father had passed. Kennedy Harlow was being the usual pain in my ass, but Edison and Casper both shook my hand and said we still had a peaceful alliance. So why have they kidnapped and beaten us?

"Casper." I nod back, keeping my thoughts to myself.

"Confused?" Casper asks, cocking his head.

"Surprised," I answer truthfully.

Casper smiles and nods as if satisfied with my answer.

The door bangs again in the silence and another figure joins Casper at his left side.

Edison Ramon.

"I know you're familiar with my cousin, so I'll skip the introductions," Casper says, patting Edison on the shoulder.

They stand united together, a familiar stance I know well as I have the same relationship with Dax.

"It's been a long twenty-six years waiting for this moment," Casper says.

I look him up and down, and Casper smiles.

"See any similarities?" He laughs.

"What the fuck do you want, Ramon? Edison, what the fuck is this?" I spit, looking at Edison for answers. Only he doesn't answer. Casper does.

"Funny story for you, King. You see, Edison doesn't run the Third District. I do. He's the face of the District, makes it look like he's running things, but he isn't."

"Why? If you're running it, why do you have to hide behind Edison?" I question, trying to piece together where he's going with this.

"All in good time, my boy." He hits my shoulder before he continues. "When my father died, way before you were born, Carlo Rhivers was running things at the Third until I became old enough to start pulling the strings. Carlo taught me the trade and helped me get started before leaving me to my own devices. I had regular meetings with your parents. They were quite fond of me and liked to think they'd raised me into the leader I am today. Carlo liked to try and take credit. I was a young lad, so naturally, my ego was big and I was proud and I hated the fact he was taking credit for the things I was doing.

"However, one day, your father had to go out of town for something and our meeting was cut short. I was at the Rhivers mansion with your mother. Let's just say Emily was very fond of me. Younger and more charming than her husband, a powerful man," he said, a sparkle of evil shining behind his eyes.

"What are you saying?" I spit out, rage blinding me.

"I had an affair with your mother, King. God, she was obsessed with me. Whenever Carlo was out of town, she'd find me and we'd have endless sex until the day your father returned." He smiles a wicked smile as I squirm in my seat. "Only we were stupid and a few times we didn't use protection. Twelve weeks later, we discovered she was pregnant. Carlo was thrilled. Six months later, you were born and for a year our lives continued as normal. Emily raised her son with Carlo whilst continuing to have an affair with me. You, however, looked nothing like your father and he started to become suspicious of your mother's behaviour. When she disappeared for too long at a time or refused to sleep with him.

"Carlo wasn't stupid and he put two and two together. Your mother confessed her love for me. I admitted to the affair and my growing feelings for your mother. As punishment, he raped and knocked her up, waited until the baby was born, only to find out it was a girl. So, he murdered Emily, his own wife, and took my leadership off me and gave it to Edison here," Casper says calmly, pointing to Edison at his side.

My blood boils as I go over the truth of my life. Carlo isn't my father but Casper is? Bonnie was a baby born from rape by my father? Carlo had actually murdered my mother, meaning he was solely responsible for the reason why I no longer had a mother or a sister.

Casper continues on as if my rage is nothing.

"Of course, we put up the front that Edison was in

charge when we'd really had this pretence all along. We were going to kill Carlo eventually for everything he'd done. But because of the position your father was in and the fact he'd demoted me from leadership, it took me years to finally get to him. Twenty-three years I waited. I went to see him to end his life once and for all. He was hosting a large District party, but I'd cornered him in his study and we got into an argument. I told him I would end his life for murdering Emily. Only there was a shadow that moved from underneath the door and when Carlo opened it, we discovered Mrs Elisa Harlow rushing down the hallway."

I chance a look at Theo, whose eyes narrow at the mention of her mother.

"Carlo shouted something ridiculous about eavesdropping and consequences, and I seized my chance and made a deal with Carlo. Elisa's life for yours, King. At least this way I'd have some sort of relationship with my son. Only once I'd drowned Elisa in her bathtub, Carlo went back on his word, so I had to get Kennedy involved."

"*You* killed my mother?" Theo shouts and I glance back at her to see her face red with rage, her knuckles white from where she grips onto the armrests of the chair with fresh tears in her eyes.

"Yes, Theodora," Casper says, shrugging one shoulder. "I then approached your father and told him Carlo had murdered her. I needed as many people on my side, you see. Kennedy was only too eager to help take Carlo down, not just for 'murdering his wife' but because of all the power he had over all of us.

"Only you, little Miss Harlow, put a spanner in the works. Kennedy had said you were adamant that your mother was murdered and refused to believe the story of her drowning. So I made a new deal."

My mind runs a mile a minute as I try to figure out what the fuck I'm going to do now. How am I going to get Theo out of this? Casper turns to Theo and brings his story to a conclusion.

"Your father was in the process of selling you to me so I could deal with you appropriately. To kill you, maybe have a little fun in between." He drools and I visibly shake in my chair at the thought of him anywhere near her. "But then you went and murdered Carlo—thank you, by the way—and then ended up in King's clutches and inside that fucking prison."

Casper stops and lets us take it all in, standing there silently, hands in his pockets, as if he just told us a fairy tale.

"On that note, I thought you were in prison, hmm?" Casper asks, looking at Theo.

She flinches and her gaze comes back to me.

"Word got back to me that my hit hadn't succeeded, so I tried again, only my inside man said you were gone. I assumed you'd be at King's, so I've waited for you, Miss Harlow, and here we are." He smiles wide.

"You were behind the anonymous payments into Kennedy's account? 'For the girl'. That was intended for Theo?" I ask, seeking clarification.

"Yes, I stopped paying him when I realised he wasn't giving me her. So to speed things up, I decided to just kill her whilst she was inside and rinse Harlow of his money for not following through on our deal."

"You're sick," Theo spits, glaring at Casper.

"I see King here is just as sick as his so-called father,

always wanting what's not his. I suppose we could share, Son?"

I shake in my chair and spit right in his face.

"I will never be your son. And you will never touch Theo."

"Is that a challenge?" he questions, stepping up to Theo and trailing a finger down her cheek.

She jerks away from him, cringing at his touch and probably the ache in her body that's still there from the car hit.

Casper traces his finger all the way down her cheek and across her lips, until Theo bites down and Casper yanks his hand back, swings it round, and smacks her right across the cheek.

Her face jerks all the way to her shoulder at the impact of the slap and she hisses as his hand yanks her hair back.

"Try anything like that again, girl, and I'll start having some of that fun I was talking about earlier," he whispers in her ear. "Maybe King can watch, hmm?"

I buck against the chair, trying to shake myself out of the knots I'm tied up in, when Casper walks away from Theo and back to me.

"So what do you want now, huh?" I ask, trying to come to the conclusion of all of this.

"Well, I'm the rightful heir to the First District, I believe, now that your mother and sister are gone."

"*I'm* the heir to the First District," I spit. "Even if I'm not Carlo's son, my mother was a Rhivers. When Carlo died, the District became *mine*."

"This is all very true, but when I kill you, it will be mine, *Son*." He smiles, looking like the cat who ate the canary.

## 33. Theo

I watch Casper as he continues to talk to King, but my ears are ringing, my blood is boiling, and if I don't get out of this chair soon, I'm going to really lose my shit.

Casper Ramon killed my mother. He drowned her in our bathtub and left her there. He's the reason I don't have a mother. He's the reason I have fucking scars on my arms. He's the reason I became a coldblooded murderer in my plan of revenge against Carlo fucking Rhivers.

He didn't entirely deserve to die for killing my mother, but he deserved to die for murdering Emily and Bonnie. He should have died a long time ago.

And King was right, my father *was* planning to sell me. The fucking psychopath. He was so invested in money and claiming Carlo's death as his own that he'd sell his own daughter to someone he knew would hurt me.

And to think I was pinning all this hate and anger towards King the past couple of days, accusing him of wanting to kill me, when in reality, he's been protecting me more than I even realised this whole time, even from the moment he put me in that prison.

Casper's threat floats in the air around us when the door

opens and bangs shut once again and through the shadows my father appears to stand at Edison's side.

"Ahh, Kennedy, you made it," Casper says, opening his arms wide, gesturing to us, his two captives.

"Are you about done?" my father replies, bored almost. His eyes scan the room but never fully land on me, and he just disregards that I'm even here. I've never had the best relationship with my father and I should've known after he tossed me into King's arms all those months ago that he never really did care about me. Why should he start now?

"Kennedy, that's not a way to treat our guests now, is it?" Casper scoffs. "I was just filling our friends in about our plans. And talking of plans." Casper turns to look at him. "Do you have my money?"

I look between him and my father, raging that they're talking about this in front of me, discussing me like a transaction.

My father pinches the bridge of his nose and scrunches his eyes shut.

"No, Ramon, I told you I'm not giving anything back to you. You paid me for her, you *have* her. I didn't get my full amount anyway." He sounds exasperated as if he's so done with talking about me.

"You didn't get your full amount, Harlow, because I've had to wait months for Theodora when she should've been mine in a matter of weeks. You broke our deal, so you owe me my money back."

"Enough," King shouts, causing all three men to look at him. "I told Kennedy this way back when and I'll tell you now. Theodora is mine."

Casper smiles and looks at me before looking back at

King and down to his bloodstained shirt.

"Sure doesn't look like she wants to be yours. Maybe you're more like Carlo than I thought. Like to take what isn't yours," Casper taunts.

King growls and reels his head forward, headbutting Casper right on the nose.

"I am nothing like him. Like any of you," he spits ferociously.

As Casper recovers from the shock, wiping his nose with the back of his hand, collecting the drips of blood, Edison storms up to King and punches him square across the jaw a couple times.

King takes it like a man, not a single noise escaping his lips, nor showing pain or vulnerability. I almost scream in protest but think better of it.

"What I find amusing is how anyone thinks they have a say in anything. Theodora Harlow is in fact mine. The Districts are mine. King, son, even you are mine."

"Casper, we had a deal," my father shouts, stepping up to Casper so he's standing right in between me and King. "We run this together. You can have the girl and the kid. I don't give a fuck. But we agreed. Take out Carlo and we do this together." His dismissal should've hurt, but I'm beyond that now.

Kennedy turns his back to Casper to address Edison when a loud shot rings out through the small dark room and I'm in the front row seat to see the bullet flying straight into Kennedy Harlow's skull from behind.

My father drops instantly, blood splattering onto all of us in close proximity, and I hold my breath, trying to keep the stench of my father's dirty blood from my senses.

I don't flinch. I don't cry. I don't feel any type of remorse. I feel relieved.

My mother deserved better. I deserve better. And now that he's gone, I'm one step closer to that.

My father's cold body bleeds out on the floor at our feet. His blazer is drenched, sodden on the floor in a pool of blood, and I spot his gun tucked into his side just under the inside pocket.

My eyes lock with King's. I can tell he's trying to figure out how I'm feeling, but my blank persona is honestly how I feel on the inside.

Regret washes through me at accusing him of wanting to murder me when really he was trying to warn Kennedy off and keep me safe. He opened up to me, finally gave in and let me in, and I betrayed him, not trusting him.

If we get out of here, I'm going to rectify that.

"Untie her," Casper says, nodding to Edison, who comes behind my back and starts sawing at the ropes with a blade. As the rope loosens, I wiggle my wrists for the freedom, trying to ease the ache in them and the burn of the rope that cuts into my skin.

Casper watches King. King watches me.

Once my arms are free, Edison holds them tight in his fists and brings his mouth to my ear.

"Try anything, and you're dead."

I nod my understanding and when he lets go of my wrists, I bring them around to my chest and rub at each wrist.

"Stop," Casper says, looking over his shoulder at us, just as Edison was about to get to work on the ropes restraining my ankles.

Edison freezes and stands up, his brows drawn together in confusion.

Casper looks back at King, who still hasn't taken his eyes away from me. His eyes flicker to the floor, at Kennedy's body, then back up to me. I follow his gaze to the gun under Kennedy's blazer, knowing he's too far away for me to reach. I'd be dead before I even tried.

"You might hate to admit it, boy, but you're a lot like me. Falling for the girl who shouldn't be yours," Casper says to King as his eyes leave mine to look at his.

"She is mine," King simply replies, gritting his teeth.

"She might have been once," he says, then takes slow steps backwards until he's next to me.

Casper walks behind me, but I keep my focus ahead, looking at nothing but King. Casper's hands come around my neck and he collects my hair, gathering it into one hand and pulling any stray strands out of my face.

He pulls my hair back, exposing my neck, and I clench my fists, ready to punch him as soon as he makes any wrong move. King's fists hold on to the armrests of the chair tightly, mirroring my actions.

"Edison." Casper nods and before I can do anything, Edison has my hands held in his firm grip behind my back again.

I yank my arms and scratch at his hands, but I'm not strong enough and Edison's hold remains firm around my wrists.

Casper comes in front of me and bends down, his face level with my stomach between my parted legs. I keep my head held high but look down my nose at him with pure disgust.

"Shall we see what's got lover boy so worked up over you, hmm?" he taunts, fumbling with the button to my jeans.

"Go to hell." I spit directly into his eye.

He laughs and wipes my saliva away, then his hands return to my button. I thrash my hips and try to free my arms from Edison, but nothing works. Casper has successfully undone my jeans and managed to wrangle them down my legs, leaving my skin exposed, my open legs showing him my simple black knickers covering my modesty.

"Don't fucking touch her," King growls, thrashing in his seat himself, helpless.

Casper doesn't turn around or even acknowledge that King has spoken and his fingers trail up my thighs as I desperately try to shut my legs.

Casper's fingers reach my knickers and his cold fingertips pull them aside as my pussy is exposed to him.

"GET THE FUCK OFF ME!" I shout and scream, trying to jolt my hips. But nothing works. My legs are splayed open, bound to the chair with no leeway to close them.

"Theo," King whispers and my eyes find his.

As soon as I latch onto his eyes, a cold finger trails along my slit and my eyes fog, tears blurring my vision. But I keep them attached to King's and the sad helplessness glossing them.

Memories of being assaulted in the prison come back to me and I relive the whole experience but only ten times worse.

King can't protect me now. And worse, he has to watch it happen and can do nothing about it.

I blink to clear the tears from my eyes and take a deep

breath in as Casper's finger descends lower to my entrance, when a loud bang echoes through the small room and the door flies open once again.

At the distraction, Edison's grip loosens on my wrists and I pull them free before landing a hard uppercut against Casper's chin, punching his jaw in full force. His head jerks back but only for a few seconds before he retaliates, but I'm already on him.

I lunge forward and crash into him, taking the metal chair my legs are still tied to with me. I land multiple punches anywhere I can, and even though my knuckles are killing me, I don't stop.

I can hear shouts and the sounds of grunts coming from around me, but my only focus is on Casper and the gun in my father's blazer. Casper pushes me off him and I use the momentum to push myself up with my arms and try to haul myself over to where my father's corpse is.

The chair is heavy on my ankles and the rope is searing into my skin as I try to pull myself across the floor.

Casper lands on top of me and turns the top half of my body so I'm lying on my back, my hips at a weird angle as the metal chair won't twist the lower half of my body with it.

Casper's hands find my neck, but they don't fit like King's does and he presses down hard, denying me any oxygen as they squeeze tighter and tighter.

I reach my arm above me, feeling around for the gun as my fingers trail over the sticky blood. My arm weakens as my life is drained out of me, but my fingers find the handle and I stretch as much as I can trying to get a hold of it.

"Oi, cunt!" a feminine voice shouts out and pulls at the hairs on Casper's head, hauling him up. Casper's fingers loosen the tiniest fraction around my neck, and with the little strength I have left, I palm the handle of the gun and in one swift motion, bring my arm down, directly in front of me, and shoot, and for the second time in only a matter of months, I fly a bullet straight through the skull of evil.

Casper's body goes limp, his blood coating my skin, mixing with the remains of my father's and he falls forwards towards me before a boot flies across me and kicks him off to collapse at my side.

I throw the gun to the floor and reach for my neck with shaky hands, trying to alleviate the pressure and take huge gulps of air back into my lungs.

"You okay?" Rori says, wincing at her stupid question, crouching down next to me and holding out her hand in comfort. I hold on to it and as I sit up I realise my ankles have been cut free from the ropes. Deep red gashes surround them, blood dripping harshly and pooling on the floor. My bare legs are scraped from the floor and covered in bruises from the car hit.

I'm a fucking mess, but I'm alive.

Rori helps me stand and I wince at the pain in my ribs and ankles, whilst trying to gain my balance. Once steady on my feet, Rori is at my side, holding my hand, and I look ahead to see Edison on the ground, King and Dax standing united in front of us.

Four people who should have never been part of each other's lives, but by circumstance ended up being the only people they needed. Four people, battered and bruised, moulded by their past, united together in an odd harmony.

I've never known the feeling of family, but I do now.

# Epilogue
## Theo

I stare out at the forested area in front of the huge floor-to-ceiling windows, remembering the last time I was here. I'd been assaulted by one of the inmates. King, Dax, and Puck had come to my rescue.

Puck.

It seems longer than a year that I was in here with him, living out every day as it came. It feels like yesterday that I would talk to him for hours, predicting the weather, laughing at his stories about King, crying at his stories about Bonnie.

I place my hands on the cool glass, my head in between them, looking out at the rain falling heavily outside. I close my eyes and listen as the rain hits the window, trying to keep my own tears at bay and let the sky cry for me like it did that dreadful night.

I hate closing my eyes when I'm alone.

I feel the pain of everything.

Of losing my mother, the assault, losing Puck, finding out about the horrifying fate my father had in store for me, Casper's cold fingers trailing over my skin.

My arms heat up and my ankles burn as the thoughts come creeping back. I've never had any phantom pains from the burns on my arms, but since my ankles were badly cut and scarred from the rope, I feel it.

My arms feel like they're on fire and my ankles feel like they're being pricked by a million needles. The pain leaves when I open my eyes, but sometimes it's too hard, and I drown with my demons in the black abyss behind my eyelids.

Until the same voice brings me back to earth, to the light of day and my protector. Every time.

"Theo," King whispers, caging me in and placing his palms against mine on the window.

My eyes flutter open and I take in the forest and the raindrops on the window. The condensation fogging the view as I breathe heavily against it. It feels so much like before when I first discovered King had been a prisoner here that I can't believe any time has passed at all.

"Is he dead?" I ask, turning my head to the side. King nods, a small smile playing on both of our lips.

Eight months ago, Dax and Rori found us in a basement buried somewhere in the Third District. They heard the commotion outside of me getting hit by Casper's car and Dax checked the security footage. They tracked the car's number plate only to discover it had been stolen and abandoned amongst a retail park of empty warehouses, so after hours of following the only other set of tyre tracks in the vicinity, they'd finally discovered us hidden underground in one of them.

However, Edison Ramon had survived his very brutal hit to the head. But instead of finishing the job, I suggested locking him away to rot. Only word got around the prison that Edison Ramon had in fact been working with Casper, who was responsible for the hit on me in the prison, and in that case, responsible for Puck's death too.

So Edison suffered eight long months of torture and trouble at the District Prison by the many loyal friends of Puck, only for our dear friends, Sandy, Mac, and Ty to finish him off for good.

I'm glad they got their form of revenge for their friend just like I did.

King had returned to clear the mess and see for himself the remains of Edison Ramon's body and I tagged along, wanting to feel close to Puck.

He would have loved the way the Districts live now. The Rhivers cousins took over all three Districts for good. Just one leader for all, to solve the issue of betrayal and power-hungry assholes.

King and Dax run them as one with Rori's and my support.

Rori Rhivers, now married to Dax, which was, in her words, 'about fucking time', has become my closest friend and ally and without fail brings me back to the here and now when my mind takes me elsewhere.

She's battled many demons of her own and finally has someone to share it all with. It's taken time, but me and Rori are thick as thieves, and I trust her with my whole life.

Oh, and we also replaced the family portrait on the wall.

"Are you ready to go?" I ask King softly, trying to turn in his arms, but he keeps me trapped against the window.

"Almost," he replies, bringing his arm back in front of my face to reveal a small velvet box.

I look at it, then at King, then back at the box. King slowly opens it to reveal a sparkling ring, silver diamonds wrapped around the band with a light blue diamond in the centre.

"Theodora, you are the brightest light of my life. The blue in my sky, the blue in my waterfall. The blue eyes that open up to me every day you wake, every time you come back from your dark place. I want to be the blue in your life. The blue of your sky, the blue of your waterfall, the blue in your diamonds," he says, lifting the ring out of the box and slowly pushing it down my finger. The blue diamond catches the last of the light outside, the raindrops reflecting off of it on the window.

I hold my hand out in front of my face, resting it against the window from where King keeps me pressed against it, admiring the gorgeous ring and the words of the man who gave it to me.

"Are you with me, Theodora? Can I be your blue? Do you want me to be?" he whispers, waiting for my answer.

And as my eyes blur from my tears and the window in front fogs from my deep breaths, I use my finger to write two simple words in the condensation on the window from my breath, like King did with me all those months ago.

I do.


THE END.

# Coming Soon

Kings of the First District: Book Two

*Rori*

He emerged from the dark like a beacon of light.
Finding me.
Saving me.
Giving me everything I want.
But not what I truly need.

*Dax*

She was lost and didn't want to be found.
But she can't hide from me.
My little bird wants to fly free.
But I'm going to clip her wings.
Doesn't she know there's no such thing as freedom?

# Acknowledgements

Firstly if you've got this far, thank you thank you thank you. This is about to get rather long and soppy, which is already cringing me out so please bare with me haha!

Carys, you get my first ever acknowledgement (yes I know, your new claim to fame, you're welcome!) You were the first person I told about Prisoner and you have been non-stop supportive since that day. I love you and I'm sorry it's taking me so long to give you Dax and Rori, but they're coming! Thank you for being you.

Helen, alongside Carys you read Prisoner in screenshots. SCREENSHOTS! You both put up with months and months of random screenshots of each chapter until the book was done. You've been amazing in this whole process, from giving me random days off to write or just hyping me up daily. Thank you!!

Katie, where do I bloody start with you. I would be literally nowhere without you. And I'm not exaggerating. You have kept me afloat this whole damn time and literally baby stepped me the whole way without complaint. I mean, I still have absolutely no idea what I'm doing but I'm not worried because I have YOU. Thank you for being such an amazing friend and never once let me get buried under my panicky moments. Here's to many more books together where I never leave you alone... Sorry in advance haha!!

Billie. Thank you for literally BULLYING me throughout this whole process haha!! You have pushed and pushed me from the start and it's been exactly what I needed. You were my first official author reader and it scared the absolute crap out of me but you've been one of my biggest supporters since day one and I couldn't appreciate you more. You're a legend.

Lauren, I'm sorry I've mentioned you fifth here but you know you're my number one in life!! I have never been more terrified to tell someone I was writing this book. I don't know why but I was. We used to really joke about it but shit got really serious. Thank you for always supporting me, loving King and Theo's story and reading everything I recommend to you. And you can tell all your friends at work that yes, this is porn... And what!!! You're my bestie, I love you forever.

Mum, you are the absolute best. I know writing this book was super random but you've encouraged me every step of the way. And even though it embarrasses me when you hype it up to our family and your friends, I still couldn't ask for a better cheerleader on my side. Also thanks for not making it awkward that you're reading the sex I've written haha!

Courtney, even though you couldn't read Prisoner straight away you got round to it and I'm still not over the reaction and love you have for it. Thank you for always being you, being a booksta bestie and sticking by me on this random venture I've decided to take. I love you. And thank you to your incredible nan. She was a fabulous beta reader for me and I appreciate her comments so much. Also sorry Lesley, but King kept his fedora hat, please forgive me!

Megan, it still baffles my brain everyday that you decided to make me merch and hype me and Prisoner up MONTHS before I was doing anything with it. You've literally been one of the best hype girls ever and I am so grateful and so appreciative of you. Also I am so sorry about Puck, I know how much you loved him. I promise I'll try and make it up to you!

Barnsley, you were my first beta reader and I am forever thankful to you. I bombarded you out of the blue and didn't really give you a choice. Thank you for always voicenoting me and being a real one.

Zoe, you probably still haven't read Prisoner but that's okay because you're my booksta bestie and I wouldn't have got this far without you anyway. I love you lots.

Cassie, you are a legend. You followed Elsspages in the early days and have hyped up my bookstagram journey from the beginning and you've been so excited for me and Prisoner ever since. Thank you for always talking books with me at work!!!

To my ARC readers. You are legends. Thank you for taking a chance on a newbie author and diving into Prisoner. I hope you stick around for more.

Emily, thank you for being a wonderful editor and putting up with my amateur ass. You've made this experience so smooth and I am so grateful.

Kirsty, I am so in love with my cover and even though it was a long wait it was totally worth it. Thank you also for making this process easy and fun for a newbie.

RuNyx, your Dark Verse series inspired this story from me. I'd recently finished reading The Reaper and I was having a major breakdown one night and I was thinking about your books and bam… Prisoner came to light. Would this story have come to me eventually one day if I hadn't read the Dark Verse? Sure maybe. But it was your words that inspired me in the first place and I will forever be grateful for the escapism and love I have for you and your stories. Thank you for giving me and many others the love of your books, but thank you for helping me find my voice.

And lastly to you, my reader. I cannot believe you finished my book, and christ I hope you liked it. But even if you didn't, that's okay too. I wrote this book for ME and I published it because I was, well, pretty much harassed lol. But it was time I shared it with the world. And for good or for bad, I appreciate you and the time you've given me and my story. Thank you.

# About Ellie Kent

Ellie is a twenty-six year old girl from Cheltenham who lives and breathes dark romance. She's always been a reader and her life revolves around indie authors, so decided to take a leap of faith and join them all in this writing journey.
Aside from reading and writing Ellie loves to bombard her friends and family and force them to spend time with her. She loves the theatre and musicals and will sing and dance anywhere and everywhere.
She's loud as fuck and rarely gets embarrassed but that's why people love her.

Head over to Facebook and join Ellie Kent's Captives at www.facebook.com/groups/elliekentscaptives

facebook.com/elliekentauthor
instagram.com/elliekentauthor

*Also by
Ellie Kent*

**Kings of the First District:**

Prisoner

Book Two (Coming Soon)

Book Three (Coming Later Than Soon)

Printed in Great Britain
by Amazon

10787231R00164